Verge 2019

Verge 2019

Uncanny

Edited by Stephen Downes, Calvin Fung
and Amaryllis Gacioppo

MONASH University
Publishing

Verge 2019: Uncanny

© Copyright 2019

Copyright of the individual works is held by their respective authors.

Copyright of the collection in its entirety is held by the editors.

All rights reserved. Apart from any uses permitted by Australia's Copyright Act 1968, no part of this book may be reproduced by any process without prior written permission from the copyright owners. Inquiries should be directed to the publisher.

Monash University Publishing
Matheson Library and Information Services Building
40 Exhibition Walk
Monash University
Clayton, Victoria 3800, Australia
www.publishing.monash.edu

Monash University Publishing brings to the world publications which advance the best traditions of humane and enlightened thought.

Monash University Publishing titles pass through a rigorous process of independent peer review.

ISBN: 9781925835373 (paperback)

www.publishing.monash.edu/books/verge2019-9781925835373.html

Series: Verge – Creative Writing

Design: Les Thomas

Cover image: Royalty-free stock photo from Shutterstock. Photo ID 269590049, by apiguide.

A catalogue record for this book is available from the National Library of Australia.

Printed in Australia by Griffin Press an Accredited ISO AS/NZS 14001:2004 Environmental Management System printer.

The paper this book is printed on is certified against the Forest Stewardship Council ® Standards. Griffin Press holds FSC chain of custody certification SGS-COC-005088. FSC promotes environmentally responsible, socially beneficial and economically viable management of the world's forests.

Contents

Foreword

The theme for *Verge 2019* came to us in an uncanny way. Among our first jobs was brainstorming a motif. One of us had just submitted a PhD thesis on the uncanny in the prose fictions of W. G. Sebald. But he was mute.

Another of our trio—we're unsure who—said, 'Why not the uncanny.' Just like that. Why not, indeed. Within seconds, we had all agreed on it. Enthusiastically. One of us remarked on the scope it gave writers. I mean, she said, think of all the strange coincidences in life, the doubles we spot in the street, the inexplicable. A student of the Gothic, another said he loved the idea for its weird and supernatural potential. The thesis writer said he thought it was a great get; he could bring a little theory to the project.

For all its commonplaceness, writers and thinkers have had trouble pinning down the uncanny. It's a concept that takes things way beyond the kind of spookiness in Mary Shelley's *Frankenstein*, perhaps the most famous monster story. In 1906, the German psychiatrist Ernst Jentsch said that someone in an uncanny situation was not quite at home, he or she lacked orientation and suffered from 'psychical uncertainties.'

Thirteen years later, Sigmund Freud wrote an essay called *The Uncanny* in which he more or less apologised for having a go at trying to understand it. The phenomenon went far beyond Jentsch's aspect of 'intellectual uncertainty,' he wrote. Freud decided that it was more to do with the involuntary emergence of thoughts and ideas that had been familiar and were repressed. (Repression was his shtick, after all.) Freud also shopping-listed other characteristics of the uncanny: coincidence, ambiguity, repetition, doubles, the dead, ghosts, severed limbs and weird 'animistic' notions that even our sophisticated psyches had trouble discounting.

Then along came British writer and academic Nicholas Royle in 2003 to enlarge the uncanny's scope even further. Critical of Freud's essay, he said that it failed to conform to its own specified principles. He thought that the hallmark of the uncanny was Jentsch's intellectual uncertainty. Freud tried to nail down the uncanny, he writes, but he couldn't do it. Moreover, it can't be done.

Most importantly, Jentsch, Freud and Royle all had things to say about the importance of the uncanny for creative writing. The uncanny allowed authors to make readers believe things that were unworldly and other-worldly. Echoing the American academic and critic Harold Bloom, Royle said that all great writing was great because it was uncanny. The most sublime works of literature speak to us in foreign tongues that somehow or other we understand.

Our theme, at any rate, must have been popular, because it drew a host of submissions. We've selected thirty or so for the anthology. In the main, they are short—and even shorter—stories. There are several poems. You'll meet a man who went to Bunnings to buy god, a girl who discovers that she's a wind-up doll, a poet who bought earless donkeys, and a flash of white light that saves a woman from being killed by a car.

Included in this issue are commissioned works by the winners of the Monash Undergraduate Prize for Creative Writing 2018. It's a first for *Verge*. The editors had the pleasure of inviting Aileen Westbrook, overall winner, and Dai-An Le, highest-placed entrant from Monash University, to produce new works of fiction on the theme of the uncanny as part of a mentorship program. You'll find their unnerving tales in the following pages.

The editors

Acknowledgements

The editors would like to acknowledge that this publication was created on the stolen land of the Kulin Nations, and we pay our respect to Elders past and present.

This publication would not have been possible without the time, assistance and guidance of many individuals. We'd like to extend our gratitude and appreciation to:

Dr Ali Alizadeh, Verge Coordinator and 2019 Emerging Writers' Festival Liaison

Dr Melinda Harvey, 2018 Emerging Writers' Festival Liaison

Associate Professor Simone Murray, Director of the Literary and Cultural Studies Graduate Program

Professor Robin Gerster, former Director of the Literary and Cultural Studies Graduate Program

Sally Riley, Graduate Research Administrator of the Literary and Cultural Studies Graduate Program

Dr Nathan Hollier, Monash University Publishing

Joanne Mullins, Monash University Publishing

Les Thomas, Monash University Publishing

Izzy Roberts-Orr, Emerging Writers' Festival

Will Dawson, Emerging Writers' Festival

Linh Nguyen, Emerging Writers' Festival

We would like to thank our peer-reviewers, who generously volunteered their time, effort, and expertise to reading and critically appraising the pieces featured in this publication. Thank you to:

Dr Ali Alizadeh
Dr Benjamin Andréo
Dr Daniel Baker
Dr Kate Brabon
Dr John Hawke

Dr Rebecca Jones
Dr Laura Lori
Dr Laura-Jane Maher
Dr Andrew McLeod
Dr Michelle Smith
Dr Alix Watkins
Dr Christiane Weller

Special thanks also to Ande Cunningham for the use of his photography for *Verge*'s publicity.

Our deepest gratitude goes to our contributors. It has been our pleasure to work with the talented writers featured in this anthology. Thank you for sharing your stories with us; it is our honour to bring them into the world.

Like Mouths, Like Tongues

Liz Allan

The Machine does not stop. Not under any circumstances. Not if Maria Constano, while showing off her engagement ring, accidentally waves it too close to the blade and the tiny little diamond and the finger wearing it goes up, up, up into the Machine's mouth. Not if a pregnant Adoa Contee faints to the floor at the sight of a little cow foetus sliding down the conveyor belt towards her, its bloodied umbilical cord trailing along behind it. Not even if Harry Chin falls into the rendering trough and is quickly transformed from human being into lard.

The Machine is always hungry, demanding more, more, more. If we are too slow its bellow becomes a scream, high-pitched and desperate to be filled. But if we give it too much it will cough and gag, swollen with meat and gristle.

It is a Machine, but more than that. It lives. It breathes.

We live and breathe with it.

I'm just saying he seems like a nice guy.

And I'm just saying don't put all your eggs in one basket.

We speak in hushed voices. The factory has been very quiet since The Machine took Sophie Chang.

Douche alert, somebody whispers, and we stop talking as Derek approaches. He squints as he checks our workbench for cleanliness, his eyes shrinking to pinpricks behind his glasses.

Seriously, Talia, Anna says, when Derek moves on to the next station. What's so good about this *ragazzo*?

I ponder her question as my hands snatch and grab the steak cutlets, dropping them into their containers.

He's the sort of man who keeps his word. *Affidabile.*

Anna's big brown eyes are wide. You know this after only a few weeks?

And look at her, Ying says. Gaga already.

I blush, because it's true.

Be careful, *bella*, Anna warns. You fall head over heels; ruin a nice pair of shoes.

All the women laugh and share knowing looks. They think because I'm young I don't know anything, but I know more than they think.

I will be maid of honour at your wedding, Anna announces, and I agree because she's my best friend.

But only four months later, the Machine takes Anna too.

Returning home from a nine-hour shift, I haul my aching body up the stairs. I sit on the front step of our unit and put my purse on my knees so the dirt doesn't stain it and I close my eyes. I block out the sounds of the neighbours, who are always cooking and yelling. I block out the whoosh of passing planes, swooping so low the wind chimes rattle.

On the other side of the door, Carla and Marco wait. They need dinner and bathing and help with their homework, and Mum will not be home until morning. When I open the door they will be my responsibility. But for now I'm just a normal girl.

Hey, beautiful, Richard answers, when I call him. Just the sound of his voice makes me nervous, so I prattle about my day.

Move in with me, Richard says. You deserve better than rotting in that factory, in that flat.

I lean my head against the door and listen to the steady humming of the neighbour's air conditioner. I imagine what it would be like to live with Richard and then I think of Carla and Marco, eating cereal for dinner in the blue glow of the television.

My mother needs my help.

Doesn't she have a man?

I haven't told Richard about Stefan. When he staggers in late at night I sneak into the kid's room and sleep on the floor.

The neighbour's air conditioner rattles and groans, sounding just like the Machine. When I sleep, I dream of its silver shell. The Machine has many openings like mouths, and the mouths have many conveyor belts, like tongues. Sometimes, in my nightmares, the flesh is stripped from my bones and I am thrown into the Machine like an animal. But lately the dream has changed a little, so that Richard waits at the end of the conveyor belt. He takes all the ruined parts of me and puts them back together again.

We call it Hog Fog, the sickness some people get from the pork. It starts with an itchy, peeling rash that leaves craters on your chest and neck. For some people, the rash starts inside their heads, making their eyes pink and leaking pus. After that they get headaches and chest pains; they have trouble breathing and stop work to bend over, concentrating on drawing breath. They forget things, like how to use the scales and what buttons to press on the control panels. When she got sick Edith Marvino forgot where the staff room was. Jay Martinez forgot how to get home from the factory. Abu Hanifa forgot to chock the forklift wheels and crushed Deepa Patel into the wall.

If one of us gets a headache or feels tired or grumpy, we check our skin and eyes for signs. If someone gets a rash we tell them to go to a doctor right away. If someone forgets their own name we call their partner to come and pick them up immediately.

It's usually too late by then.

I walk through the boning hall with a smile. Normally, the stark walls and swinging carcasses depress me but today I wave happily at the butchers, thinking about Richard.

What about Carla and Marco? Anna asks, when I tell the girls what he said.

They can visit. Richard loves kids; he has two of his own already.

So, what? Anna raises her eyebrows. You're going to move in with Richard, raise his *bambini* instead of your mothers'?

If you two don't shut up you'll get cleaning duty, Ying hisses.

Derek scans our workstation with his beady eyes. Moving on to the next station, he stops behind the new girl.

We have increased to forty-three hundred carcasses per day, and not everyone is keeping up.

The new girl unties her tunic as Derek escorts her into his office. Everyone on the factory floor lifts their head to watch. I feel bad for her but also relieved.

3

We're still talking about the new girl when The Machine coughs and splutters. We freeze as men come running from all corners and the orange lights start to flash.

Heads down, Ying says, keep going. We watch the men shouting and running while our hands continue packing the cutlets into the trays.

A second later, the Machine stops altogether. The lights change from orange to red and we press our hands to our ears as the alarm starts to ring and then changes to a WHOOP. The Machine roars: a gargled, choking sound that makes the floor tremble. We drop and crawl underneath our workstations as the window glass starts to shatter and the Machine's roar becomes a scream. We huddle close to each other, our mouths moving in prayer as the earth opens up underneath us.

* * *

When Derek taps me on the shoulder the next day I hear a gasp and I don't know if its Anna's or mine. I follow Derek through retail and out into the trimming hall, smelling the stink of my own fear sweat. I keep my head down and my eyes lowered but I hear people whisper as we pass.

Another packer, Cindy, waits in his office. I take the chair next to hers.

You know that we are always watching you, Derek says, staring at a spot above our heads.

I'm a very hard worker, Cindy says. I had surgery last week.

I don't care. Everyone is replaceable.

I fold my hands in my lap so I don't leave sweat marks on the armrests. I think of the overdue electricity bill and the empty kitchen cupboards; Carla's upcoming excursion and the holes in Marco's shoes. I pray I'm being demoted instead of fired. If I get sent to cleaning duty there's always a chance I can work my way up again, provided nothing happens.

You've been selected for administration traineeships, Derek says.

I nearly fall out of my chair. Cindy screams and claps her hands but the clap is silent because she's still wearing her mesh gloves.

This is a government initiative, it's not my choice, Derek says when I try to thank him. You will have to move to Newcastle, he adds.

I return to the workstation and Anna grabs my wrist, her gloved fingers tight as a bracelet. My eyes are filling up but I don't let myself cry.

I'm ok, I tell her, and she returns to her work, accepting my lie without question.

Look at you, look at you, Richard murmurs, when I answer the door. I'm wearing one of Anna's little black dresses, and I spent hours scrubbing so I would smell like soap for once. I shut the door carefully so I don't wake the children. Once we get to the bottom of the stairs, I feel a weight slide off of my shoulders.

He takes me to Popolo, and the candlelight makes his dark eyes glitter like stars. I stammer, intimidated by the wait staff, and then ask for the fish.

Pesce, Richard corrects, smiling at the waiter. He is so sophisticated, not like the idiots my mother dates.

Richard, I say, and his gaze fixes on me, the sparkle in his eyes suddenly dimming. My throat is dry and I struggle to get the words out.

I've been offered an administration traineeship.

His face lights up. That's *wonderful*.

I have to move to Newcastle.

I watch nervously as Richard stares down at the table, his eyes fixed on his napkin.

That's wonderful, he repeats, finally looking up at me. The bright smile has returned and his eyes are soft, even proud.

The contaminated pork comes from Smithson Farm, where the cages are too small for the pigs to turn around. It's one hundred degrees in the warehouses and there's no sunlight, no straw, no fresh air or earth. The animals are so confined that they trample each other to death.

We don't know what causes Hog Fog exactly but we know that the farmers pump the pigs with antibiotics to keep them alive long enough to be slaughtered. We know that the meat coming into The Machine is full of microbes and parasites and fungi and vaccines and ammonia and methane and carbon monoxide and cyanide. Sometimes I smell the pig's terror in my own skin, a sweet and sour stench of shit and blood and fear. Sometimes I think that's the real sound the Machine makes: animals, screaming and dying.

I'm drunk by the time we return home and Richard laughs as I kick off my heels in the doorway. I think Richard is drunk as well because by the time we finish my butt and thighs are reddened with handprints.

He slides off of me and props himself on one elbow.

You're so sexy, he says. It's such a shame you're moving away.

My body breaks out in a cold sweat. I push myself up to sitting.

Come on, Talia. He turns over to retrieve his glass of wine. I've got two kids here and a business to run. You think I have time to drive back and forth between here and Newcastle?

But… I accept the wine glass he offers, my hands shaking so hard I almost drop it. I can drive some of the time. It's not that far.

Honey, Richard kisses me gently on the forehead. I can't say I'm not disappointed. But you have to do what's right for you.

A high, ringing noise starts in my ears, like the sound of the alarm before it changes. I look down at his handprints on my skin and feel old and used up, the way my mother looks. When I was little I watched her worship men like Gods. Men who didn't deserve her attention, men whose needs were always put before my own. I promised myself that I would never be weak like her, never the servant or the slave.

The Machine must be kept juicy and moist with enough animal parts in circulation and just the right consistency of liquid to solid. If we are too slow and the Machine becomes empty it screams out to be filled, and I too, know that emptiness, that feeling that there is a pit inside your belly and its pink and slippery walls only widen with every breath so that eventually all that emptiness consumes everything and the pit is all that remains of you.

The next time the alarm sounds I watch all of the girls hide under their workstations. Instead of covering my ears I turn towards the Machine and listen. Before Anna grabs me and pulls me down to the floor I realise that the Machine's roar is not one of anger, but of grief.

You're joking, Anna says.

It's not a big deal.

Not a big deal? Giving up an opportunity like that?

Nonna always said that jobs come and go, but *la famiglia e'per sempre*, I reply, smugly.

Famiglia? Anna laughs. You're not staying for Carla and Marco. You're staying for *him*.

Hey! Ying hisses and we all go quiet as Derek approaches.

Miss Bundalo. Is there a problem?

I shake my head. His eyes are black and still.

Do you think that turning down a promotion has made you better than everyone else? Do you expect the others to pick up the slack for you now?

Derek leans in closer and I notice a red spot in his eye like a single drop of blood.

If I have to warn you again, he whispers. You will be moved to cleaning duty.

A bead of sweat runs down my sternum and I nod, exhaling once his back is turned.

You better pull it together, Ying says. Unless you want to end up like Sophie Chang.

At Smithson Farm after the sows give birth they sometimes trample their babies to death. Perhaps it is not always an accident. Perhaps it is an act of mercy.

One morning Richard comes up behind me when I am checking my eyes and skin in his bathroom mirror. I see a small pink spot in the corner of my eye, a fleck of dust maybe, but it doesn't come away when I touch it.

Anna walks into the restaurant wearing a tight leather skirt. Her mouth makes a wide 'o' when she spots us and she scuttles over, knocking the back of a woman's head with her handbag.

Niente, niente, Anna says, when I ask her what's wrong. I'm just so excited to meet your Prince Charming.

They get along well, as I knew they would. Richard keeps the wine coming all evening, and it isn't until I stand up to go to the bathroom that I realise I'm drunk. In the vanity mirror I try and fail to remove the wine stain from my mouth. When I return to the table dessert has been served and I pick up my spoon, taking a bite of my pistachio panna cotta.

Is it good? Richard smiles.

I don't think I can finish, I say. Too full.

Anna snorts. This girl has room. Just wait until she's comfortable enough around you to start eating again.

I pretend to laugh but her comment stings. The waiter asks if we want coffee, and I decline with a yawn.

We're only just getting started! Anna cries.

Richard laughs. Talia mentioned that you're a party girl.

Well, what's wrong with having a little fun? Unless you're this one, she says, pointing at me.

Hey, I say. What's with you tonight?

Her eyes are round and innocent and I realise she is jealous. It makes me pity her, and I hug Anna extra tight before she gets into the cab.

She deserves a good man, I say to Richard, as the car pulls away. Someone to take care of her.

Seems like she can take care of herself, Richard replies, and then he puts his arm around me and kisses me so deeply that I forget about Anna and everything.

We are moved to the fabrication room, where we trim hair and fat from the pork using small, handheld blades called Whizards. We stand so close our elbows touch and the Whizards cover us with gristle. Although it's freezing cold in the factory, we're all sweating. Behind us, a row of men uses bandsaws to slice up the hindquarters, hurling all of the nasty bits into buckets. The bandsaws are very close to our backs, and the screech of the blades makes it impossible for us to talk.

I put down my Whizard and turn away to cough. Anna stares in alarm as my cough goes on and on. I feel a wave of dizziness and reach out for the table but I clutch air instead, before bumping into Ying on my other side. As I hit the floor I hear a gasp, followed by a high-pitched scream.

I scramble to my knees as the safety men come. They wrap Ying's hand in cloth and usher her out of the factory. Derek comes over with a bottle of bleach to clean the blood from the equipment.

Back to work. Derek says.

Va bene, Anna says. Keep going, Talia.

I feel her cold fingers on my wrist as she guides me back into the line.

We visit Ying every Saturday. We bring her takeaway but she only likes the expensive Chinese place. Not that I can complain after costing Ying four fingers.

Once we finish eating I start coughing again. It goes on and on, until I struggle to draw breath. Ying pats me on the back, looking scared.

While Anna's in the toilet, I hear her mobile ringing.

I'll get it! I call, getting up to grab her bag from the kitchen counter.

I hear a bang in the toilet, Anna swearing, and then fiddling with the latch. I pull out her phone and look at the name on the screen. I sit down, hard, on a chair.

Talia, Anna says. Her face is white.

I drop the phone on the table as my eyes blur with tears.

I didn't mean for it to happen, she says. *Mi dispiace.*

But he loves me, I try to say. Instead of words I make a gargled, choking noise that sounds just like the Machine.

The drop of red in Derek's left eye has spread into a pool. His right eye leaks pus and the top half of a pink, itchy rash is visible on his neck above the collar.

There are so few good men in this world, Anna whispers to me. *Mi dispiace.*

I ignore her, moving my Whizard closer so the gristle sprays on her tunic.

There is no warning this time. The factory lights go bright red and the alarm goes WHOOP WHOOP WHOOP. I switch off my Whizard, reaching up to pull Anna's net from her head before grabbing hold of a fistful of her hair.

Anna screams, trying to pull her hair free while using her other hand to push me off of her. But I will not let go, and it is only once the alarm is turned off that the workers come and separate us.

The Machine has finally stopped.

A voice on the intercom tells us all to go home. A repairman is coming. We will not be paid for today.

I am removing strands of Anna's hair from my gloves when Derek comes over to tell us we're demoted to cleaning duty.

The blood and mush don't bother me but the hard stuff, the gristle: that's what I hate. I pluck a piece of it from the folds of my cloth and throw it in the bucket.

Uff, Anna says, putting down the bleach. Doesn't this smell make you think of hospitals?

I scratch at the growing rash on my neck, thinking about Sophie Chang. Sophie was the person on cleaning duty the last time the Machine stopped. *Blunt force and chopping wounds*, Ying had read on the official report.

It makes me think of hospitals, Anna says. And the *orbitorio*. Do you remember Aunt Rita's funeral? We drank *prosecco* under the stairs.

I keep scrubbing, saying nothing.

Aunt Rita told me that you can work to live or live to work. Anna stops and puts her hands on her hips. I don't think we're the kind of people who get to make that choice.

I pick up my bucket and cross over to the ladder, leaving Anna to finish her side of the Machine. I climb up carefully, making sure I don't spill my bucket.

Aunt Rita had three husbands, did you know that? Anna says. The first one was a pianist.

I climb off of the ladder and put down my bucket. I fetch a new cloth and begin cleaning the vat lid.

The second husband was a doctor, the third a lawyer. You know who she loved best? The pianist. The man with *passione* rather than money. It's so rare to find a man with both.

Something in Anna's voice makes me stop and look down at her.

Uff, she smiles, gazing up at me. Does this cleaning stuff make you dizzy? She puts a hand across her belly in an unmistakable gesture.

No? Maybe it's just me.

At the same moment that I realise she is pregnant with Richard's child, the factory door opens. The repairman walks in but he doesn't see us. I stand still behind the raised lid, not alerting him to our presence.

Anna is looking up at me from the belly of the Machine with that stupid smile still on her face. I tell her to get out of there. Or do I? My memory is so terrible, lately.

The repairman turns on the power. A groaning, grumbling sound fills the factory floor, followed by Anna's scream.

The Machine wakes.

It is hungry.

2

The Old House

Clancy Balen

A gentle scraping at the bedroom door pulled Beth out of bed. She knew it would be the old dog blind in the darkness of the early hours of the morning, letting her know he was lost. Poor sod. He had probably been sitting there all night, as usual, with the patience of a saint. Staring at nothing in particular.

Sitting up, Beth squinted in the dark. She caught her reflection in the mirror across from the bed, just a vague silhouette, fuzzy around the edges. She opened the bedroom door to find a curled-up smudge in front of her. 'You look like a little pile of rags,' she thought as she put the dog under her arm and plopped him on to the bed.

She could feel his body quiver against the morning air, so naturally she began to smooth one of his ears with her forefinger and thumb. Old, tired bones nudged into her as she felt his little body relax. Sleep was no longer going to happen, and most likely there was a puddle of dog piss to clean up outside her door, but Beth was not ready. Not until the birds started. Instead she closed her eyes and listened to the room, the laboured breathing of the dog spooned against her hip, and, ah yes right on cue, the familiar sound of her sister's snoring forcing itself in from the other room.

Beth and her sister were both in their 50's and both had recently left their partners. Beth had fallen in love as a teenager, and in unspoken solidarity her sister had done the same, something they now regarded as a bad move. Maybe it was out of love, perhaps it was out of boredom, the two sisters had found themselves married and settled before the age of 21.

The small town had lurched at the news of the double-separation and heaved when the two sisters moved back in to their old family house. Living together in middle age was not something they had planned, but when her sister Carolyn had appeared at her door on a balmy evening with a bruise near her right eye and car keys clutched in her trembling hand Beth had made the decision for the both of them. They sat and talked on the front deck that night, looking out across the dark expanse where the wetlands used to be, trying to trace the shape of the landscape they remembered over the timber frames of the half-built houses that now stood there. They played there as kids, played 'school' or 'house' using a wide, flat rock as a table. Their mother would find them when the sun went down, 'Oi, sun's down kiddos, c'mon,' cigarette in hand, pointed towards them, like a prop. Much the same way Carolyn does now, Beth thought. All of it gone now though. Their Mum passed away from a stroke a few months before, and Dad may as well have never existed.

'What are we going to do Beth?'

Beth wasn't sure. At least they still had their Mum's old house.

Depending on how you looked at it, it was lucky that they were unable to sell the house off after their mother's death. The dilapidated weather boards, the rusted tin roof. It was never meant to sell. The garage was so overladen with vines and rot that it collapsed in on itself the day before they approached the real estate agency. The spider-magnet as Beth had come to call it in her head, was a challenging feature of the house for prospective tenants. Between that and the noise from the rusted hills-hoist spinning dejectedly in the wind, it became clear that at the very least some cosmetic renovation was needed.

That was not meant to be. By the time asbestos was found in the wall paint Beth and Carolyn decided it was time to gut the whole house. This, and the garage sale that followed to help pay for it was, for Beth, akin to losing her mother all over again. All day friends, neighbours, strangers, the McCleods, the Howes, Vivian Costoletto's frail but nosey father, had come by and asked Beth to put a price on her memories.

'How much for the dresser?'

Beth's voice would catch in her throat before she could answer.

Carolyn seemed to find it hard too. 'Look at these pricks,' she had said, hands on hips, cigarette hanging limply out of her mouth. 'That old bastard worked with Mum, and still wants to barter over the fucking sofa.' Beth couldn't help but admire her sister's ability to sabotage their efforts. Carolyn spent the rest of the day practising firing lasers from her eyes into the back of unsuspecting heads. But there was a sense of achievement in doing this all by themselves. Beth had made sure that under no circumstances were their husbands to be involved. 'Carolyn, you can't ask for his help after everything that happened,' was the mantra adhered to.

By the time the house was ready to sell any trace of their childhood had been stripped away like the paint. The last patches of daylight retreated against the fresh weatherboards, patterns of dappled light settling into patterns at once both familiar and alien. Beth reassured herself that somewhere, preserved through some irreconcilable crossroad of nostalgia and neglect, their home remained. But in the present moment she could only distinguish the house with a certain colourlessness. Beth searched for some words that would offer something tangible, an assurance for the future. The afternoon continued to recede with indifference, and she swallowed her words. Instead Beth and Carolyn sat in silence on the porch, as if strangers in their own home, watching the old dog fumble amongst the newly planted seaside daises running along the fence line.

When the sisters were young the quickest way home from St. Mary's Catholic Primary School was to cut through the public-school's playground. Under God's watchful eye this was forbidden. As children Beth and Carolyn wrestled with this abstract idea by applying a steady dose of irreverence. Whether this God was benevolent or cruel, numinous or benign, mattered very little to the young girls who had not yet been taught to fear Him. They had feared Mr. McKenna, the teacher who had once taken Dennis Garland by the neck and thrown him out of class, or the groundskeeper who always smelt of alcohol on Friday afternoons. And they had feared the Grade 6 boys, who would kick a ball as high as they could into the centre of the girl's games at lunchtime. Above all they had feared Sister Marion, and her sallow hands that would grip your shoulder. Marion, Our Lady of Creative Punishments. Sister Marion, who knew an awful lot about God and the things he saw.

It was difficult to walk through the public-school without being noticed. But one day after school, when it was hot and dry, the sisters made their way to the playground. There was nothing different about that day, except perhaps a newfound determination within Carolyn to break the rules. Maybe there had been an unspoken irreverence brewing between them. There was no discussion as to why they had gone but by the time Carolyn took the lead across the unchartered tanbark, Beth felt that they were now in it together. Most of the public-school students had gone home, although some stragglers remained. Oblivious to the chance of being spotted, Carolyn made her way towards the monkey bars. Beth watched the way her sister effortlessly swung between the bars. Determined to join in she leapt at the bars but found the gaps too hard to cross. The metal of the bars in the sun burnt her hands, most badly where the paint had peeled. She fell, a small thud, the tanbark pushing in to her skin. She picked herself up and launched at the monkey bars again. In the next moment, burnt hands, a quick slip and the thud of skin hitting metal.

Beth split her chin open. She remembered the way the blood had appeared black on her dark green school dress. She remembered her sister crying and looking around for help. But most distinct was the feeling that they were on their own. No one could know they were here. Just a blur as they walked home, Carolyn holding her dress to her sister's chin to stop the bleeding and 'Oh Jesus Christ girls,' the relief she felt at their Mum's voice as they walked through the front gate. And the fear she felt the next day as Sister Marion loomed over her, a cold hand resting on her shoulder, 'You two ladies will be going to Hell for disobeying me.' Beth never could quite work how Sister Marion had found out about their trip through the public school.

Beth sat on the ugly couch in the newly furnished lounge room. The old dog was flopped in front of where the fireplace used to be. It was now an electric heater. Beth thought it looked stupid. Waving her arm to dispel the cigarette smoke floating near eyes, she attempted to muster the energy to sit up properly.

'You've been sitting like this for a while now.' Carolyn appeared in the door way.

'I've been fielding phone calls from *him* for the past few hours. I need to hit something.' Beth replied.

'What's he want?' said Carolyn.

The phone rings. They both stare at it until it stops. 'To 'talk',' Beth replied in quotation marks.

'If he calls again I am answering it for you.'

'Please, Carolyn.' Beth pressed her fingers against her forehead. 'Will you jus—?'

'How's his pet food thing going?' She was grinning now.

Beth exhaled smoke. 'Toys.'

'What?'

'Pet toys. He's selling toys for pets now.'

Carolyn cackled as she walked out of view.

'If mine ever comes around here I'll fuckin' kill 'im,' she called from another room.

Beth gave a small smile, but felt her chest tighten. She wasn't sure what would happen if he did come around. The old dog looked at her, then rolled on to its back. Beth leant forward to scratch his belly and lit another cigarette.

In the darkness Beth sat in bed and listened to the sounds of the early morning. The air was still, punctuated by the heavy breathing of the dog nestled into her side. She had decided to skip the usual routine and had let him sleep in her bed. Of course, he had pissed all over the blankets, but Beth felt philosophical this morning. In the grand scheme of things, and all that. Besides, the snoring would begin soon so staying in bed seemed like more effort than it was worth.

Bed sheets in one arm, the old blind dog under the other, Beth made her way to the laundry. A dull light had begun to creep in from the window looking out to the yard. Odd, Beth thought, that it was already light outside. Had she slept in? No snoring from Caz, what a miracle.

'Lucky us.' Beth said to the dog.

He stared back at her for a moment, then began licking himself.

Beth threw the blankets in to the washing machine but paused before beginning the cycle. She eyed the room, inspecting the new layout and fresh paint. All new. Nothing left of where she grew up really. She ran her thumb under her chin, finding the small scar and pushed on it slightly. She breathed out. And right here was where she found Mum after her stroke. God knows how long she had been lying there before she found her. Just by herself.

A noise from outside pulled Beth away, and she looked out the window. Two figures stood near the front gate, a car with its engine running sat in the driveway. Their voices were raised, a man and a woman, but Beth could not make out what they were saying. They appeared indistinct in the grey morning light, but Beth recognised her sister's shrill tone. The man grabbed her wrist and spoke quietly. Beth watched as her sister pulled away, seemed to hesitate, spoke quietly too before walking around to the passenger side door and opening it. She made a gesture, as if to challenge him. In silence, Beth watched them get in the car and pull out of the driveway, leaving her alone in the old house.

3

The Mark

Grace Chan

Things haven't been right for a few months.

I can't describe it exactly. The air is spongy, each molecule bloated with turgid energy. We've had three lightning storms this summer: dry, pounding storms without rain, purple branches crackling across a cloud-dark sky.

Several times, I've woken before sunrise, convinced that something has changed in the middle of the night. As though some god has reached down, and, with a colossal finger, nudged the Earth, and now everything is sitting two degrees off-kilter.

On these not-quite-mornings, I pad into the street in my pyjamas. I stand beneath the linked steeples of fluorescent streetlights and power lines. I scan above for the subtle movement of the clouds, to assure myself that the sky is not a two-dimensional poster glued onto a false backdrop.

One day at the end of summer, James returns from his morning run. He barrels into the bedroom, a whirlwind of breathlessness and heat, and ploughs through the drawers to find a fresh pair of jocks.

I watch him from where I lie, tangled in the too-warm sheets.

'Did you do a round of washing last night?'

'Yes,' I say. 'It's hanging in the laundry.'

He strides out of the room, returns a minute later, clutching his favourite jocks. He pulls off his sweat-soaked singlet.

'What's that?'

'What?'

'On your chest.' I point. At the base of his sternum, where bone turns to soft fleshy abdomen, his skin bears a mark like a stamp. It seems to have the muted redness of an old scar. But then it catches the light coming through the crack of the curtains, and it gleams silver.

'This?' James touches the spot absently. 'It's nothing. An old birthmark.'

'Can I see?' I sit up, but he swats me aside.

'I have to rush. It's nothing. I've had it forever. Shouldn't you be getting up too?'

He disappears into the ensuite. A few seconds later, the shower starts with a torrential roar. The pipes clatter in feeble protest. There'll be water all over the tiles, which I'll have to wipe before I go to work, or else damp will settle into the floor and we'll have mushrooms sprouting from the skirting again. Also, I need to call the plumber to check our water pressure.

James emerges and dresses in his usual uniform (tailored grey suit, white shirt, no tie) with a steadfast frenzy that characterises most of his waking hours. Somehow, in every vector of movement, he conveys to me a subtle disdain—as though, in rising an hour before me despite the lack of a fixed work schedule, he possesses a more exquisite moral fibre.

I lie in bed for another thirty minutes after he's gone. There's a strange smell in the air—sort of like bleach, and sort of like burning metal, but not quite like either. I sniff for a while, trying to figure it out, but having no success. I'm starting to get cold. I run my hands over my body, feeling the hard shape of my hips, the stagnant putty of my lower belly, which is scarred inside.

My phone buzzes. It's a message from Michelle, the other PA.

Emma—you in yet? James is here. Wants you to fix up his PM list.

In a wry coincidence, my boss's name is also James. To most of his colleagues, he goes by Jim or Jimmy. In my head I refer to him as Dr Entmore, to distinguish better his separateness, his seniority. He's a gastroenterologist. He spends four hours every afternoon negotiating the serpentine twists of the large intestine with the grim determination of a kid navigating the final level of Super Mario World. Dr Entmore refers to me as Em, or, tongue-in-cheek, the queen of his office.

I check the time: 7:51am. It'll take me twenty minutes to get ready, and half an hour to drive to the hospital in traffic. Parking will add another five minutes, and walking in another... ten?

I stall in a mire of numbers and possibilities. My mind is as sluggish as the air. I toss the phone onto the bedside table and drag myself from my stale cocoon to face the day.

* * *

That night, I'm lying in bed. James is next to me, on his back, breathing the heavy, sonorous breaths of someone in deep sleep. Moonlight comes through the crack in the curtains and falls in a grey bar across the pillows, splitting James's face in two. My husband of ten years is a stranger. I study the straight lines of his nose, which my parents always admired, and the rough plane of his cheek, which has begun to soften with age.

Gingerly, I pull back the sheets.

He doesn't stir. The mark is still there. Triangular and somehow iridescent. How could I have never noticed it before? After a decade of intimacy, his body is an extension of mine.

I peer at it closely. It's not flat, as I'd first thought, but raised around the edges, and silver as the skin of a fish. I touch it.

It's a zip.

Holding my breath, I grasp it between the pads of my thumb and forefinger. Then I pull. There is next to no resistance. The skin of my husband's torso divides soundlessly, like the front of a hoodie, revealing a black, gaping gash. I lean closer to examine what lies within, but I'm jolted by the pipes' loud banging.

I blink into the oppressive thickness of waking. I'm alone in the bed. On James's side, the quilt is flung back. His pillow is cold.

I wait for my heart to stop pounding. Gradually, sounds come to me. I hear him pacing through the house, treading a figure-eight loop from kitchen to dining room to lounge to dining room and round and round again. There's a curious rhythm to his steps.

Then I hear the tapping. Musical, light, like someone tapping a beat on the rim of a drum with a pair of chopsticks. It goes on for what feels like half an hour.

James's voice is an undercurrent to the rhythm. His murmuring ebbs and flows. I can't make out any words through the tapping noise and the buzz of electrified air. I climb out of bed and creep to the door.

I hear my name—once, then a few sentences later, again.

I step around the doorframe. James glances at me immediately. He's silhouetted by the street light pouring through the lounge room window—a lean, dark figure with no face.

'Emma,' he says.

'What's going on?' I ask. 'It's 4am.'

'Business call,' he says. 'I've got a new client in the UK.'

'I thought I heard you talking about me.'

'No,' he says. 'Business call. Sorry to wake you. Go back to sleep.'

I return to bed, dream-James and real-James swirling in my head. I roll myself so tight in the sheets I can hardly breathe, and pull the quilt over my nose. It's only as I'm drifting off to sleep that I realise my husband wasn't holding a phone.

* * *

March is a difficult month, but that's to be expected. The 8th falls on a Sunday. James is out playing tennis with his university friends. I close all the curtains and go to the second bedroom. We've converted it into a library of sorts—plush armchair with matching footstool, arranged in front of shelves of James's finance and history books. To me, though, it's still the nursery.

I still find it eerie that their deaths fell on consecutive days. That even though they were separated by three years, they tried to be close together in some way. For me, it was a double-punch to the gut—the first blow rendering me immobile for the second, the second intensifying the first. It was the ripping of a half-dried scab to expose a festering wound.

I stand in front of the chestnut dresser and open the top drawer. I take out a green shoebox. Should I light a candle? Play some meditative music? No, that seems stupid. Meaningless. They can't hear it anyway.

I lift the lid. The first item is a delicate gold anklet. My mother gave it to me, her eldest daughter. I wore it until I was twelve years old and my ankle grew too wide for it. I would have given it to Jade, if I'd kept her.

The second item is a little book of baby names. Bought on impulse from a two-dollar store, when I still wasn't sure if I'd keep her. Before James convinced me that we were too young, and it wasn't the right time.

The third item is my hospital wristband, with my name and birthdate and a seven-digit number beneath a barcode. The numbers are burned onto the inside of my skull. I muttered them over and over again as they scraped Jade out of me.

The next two items are Jasmine's. A pair of canary yellow socks, exquisitely tiny, crocheted by my maid of honour when she found out I was pregnant. Never used.

And an ultrasound still from the 12-week scan, crumpled from that day I threw it out. I'd hunted frantically through the garbage to retrieve it.

Jasmine, the wanted one, planned once James and Nish had got their firm up and running, hadn't made it to seventeen weeks. We'd lost the wanted one, you see, because we killed the unwanted one. James grieves, but not as I do. For him, the losses are cognitive, and sometimes emotional. For me, they are visceral—bloody with rage and regret.

Through penance we make amends.

I take the final item out of the green shoebox. It's an old torch, the bulb fried, with a thick corrugated cylinder for a handle. The curtains are closed. I remove my jeans and my underpants. I press the end of the torch to my vulva. Cold and dense. Through penance we heal. I make no sound as I push, even though the pain is monstrous.

* * *

On an unseasonably cold night in April, I wake in the soundless hours to discover that my husband has climbed on top of me. His weight imprints my body into the mattress. My wrists and hips ache.

His fingers fumble at my waistband.

'James,' I say, but he doesn't reply. In the wan light, I see that his eyes are glassy.

I make myself still, burrow into the recesses of my mind. The air congeals with unspent energy. As James moves over me, the mark shifts in and out of my vision. A triangle, beautiful in its symmetry. Raised around the edges and silvery-red.

* * *

Nish and his wife come for dinner, and a man I don't know, called Paul Andreski, a new business client. Paul's wife, Tara, also comes. I make roast beef with rosemary, and a grain salad. Nish and his wife bring a potato curry, which doesn't complement the meat. Paul and Tara bring a bottle of shiraz.

James tells me the day before: 'Please do your best, Emma.'

I know I haven't been myself lately. Getting through March left me exhausted. The air is so thick it's difficult to string my thoughts together. And I can't help feeling that there's something horribly wrong with my husband.

The evening gets off to a rocky start. I put the roast into the oven too late, so everyone's hungry. I cobble together a platter of sesame crackers, salmon dip, green olives that are only a little slimy. James finds a bottle of Prosecco, and the conversation starts flowing.

They talk about the cryptocurrency tumble ('only a matter of time'), the Me Too movement ('its breadth is its weakness'), and Paul and Tara's recent tour of Southern Italy ('splendid in the middle of spring'). James laughs uproariously at Paul's jokes and lavishes Tara with compliments about her knowledge of classical history. I stare at where my husband's left hand rests on the table, flat and waxy, next to his plate, creasing his napkin. It flops there like a pale fish. My own hand rests three inches away, small and dark and neat.

I move my hand, close the three inches, press our pinkies together. His skin is as cold as dead meat. James moves his hand away, unconsciously, still talking.

After dinner, I load the dishes into the dishwasher while they go to the lounge room to work on the bottle of red and a wheel of camembert. I drift to the back door. The sun has long descended behind the melaleuca trees that divide our property from the neighbour to our rear. A sweep of vivid orange holds out against the descent of the starry night. I push my toe against the fly screen, nudge it open, and step onto the back porch.

The night is cold and smells like burning fuel. At this time of year, the trees have mostly turned. Brown and yellow leaves pool across our backyard. The geraniums are drowning in weeds. The neighbour's creeper spills over the fence in a dense tangle. Usually, James would have pruned it long before it got so wild. He would have raked the leaves, too, and weeded the flower beds. I frown. He had always been an avid gardener.

I think about skin, cold as dead meat, and glassy eyes, and a triangular scar in the exact centre of the torso. The dark sky presses down on my head.

* * *

As soon as I realise the truth of it, everything falls into place. That's why, despite the utter bizarreness of the situation, I know there can be no other explanation. The electrified air, which lifts baby hairs vertically from my scalp, is charged with radio waves transmitting messages to his system. The mysterious 4am phone calls: check-ins with whichever intelligence agency has commissioned him. The triangular mark: the final stitch in his fabrication.

The house has become my territory. I clean the kitchen with a specific fierceness; I am a guard holding the outermost frontier. As I sponge the counters in firm, circular strokes, I glance through the window to the backyard. The trees are grey and bare. Rotting leaves pile up in banks against the fence, releasing a sickly-sweet scent.

He comes into the kitchen, in search of breakfast. Of course, I haven't said anything to him about my thoughts. I haven't breathed a word to anyone. I've decided to pretend that everything is normal until I figure out a sensible course of action.

I watch as he gets the box of rolled oats from the pantry, pours half a cup into a bowl, adds milk, and puts it in the microwave. As he waits for the oats to cook, he leans against the counter, tapping the spoon against his chin.

His face is not even right. That's why everything felt off-kilter. His eyebrows are dark, like they've been tattooed on. His eyes are too far apart; the contour of his hairline uniform and lacking the patches at the temples where it had begun to thin. And the two little moles beside his left nostril—completely gone.

He takes the bowl from the microwave, plunges his spoon in, and lifts it to his mouth. James would have added a carefully measured tablespoon of ironbark honey and stirred it to achieve an even distribution of sweetness.

My blood is as cold as ice. I lick my lips.

'Do you remember when we went to the hospital for Jasmine's first scan?'

He stiffens, but I push on. The memory is an ocean wave: once it has attained enough momentum, it can't be stopped. It must rise, swell, peak, crash, and be endured.

'Remember how excited the sonographer looked when she called my name—and then, when she saw me, how her smile disappeared? She was so confused.'

With a surname like Kavanagh, she'd thought she was meeting an Irish sister. She hadn't expected black hair, chestnut skin, single-lidded eyes.

He says nothing.

'Then you stood up, and the world made sense again. She adored you. Kept asking where your parents and grandparents were from. Kept saying you've got the same eyes as one of her cousins, from a town south of Cork—Bandon? Baltimore?'

'I don't remember,' he said.

His expression is blank. There is no recollection.

'How could you forget? She started implying that you'd bought me from some third-world slum. Remember?'

'No, I don't. You always read too much into these little things. She was probably just trying to be nice.'

He takes his oats to the lounge, to eat in front of the television. Even his voice sounds different. Hollow. Alien. A sensation of prickling needles rises all over my skin.

* * *

That night, I watch it sleep.

It lies flat on its back, arms by its side, like a corpse laid out on a morgue table. Eyes closed in repose, face still. Only the susurration of air moving through its nostrils, lifting the chest in gentle undulations. The fingernails look like plastic discs, glued on.

In my right hand, I clutch a metal spoon. This will confirm my suspicions, once for all.

I step closer to the bed. The silver-red mark gleams at me, tempting me to touch it and tug it and watch everything unravel.

I press the hard edge of the spoon to the soft part beneath the left eye. It sinks as easily as a knife through wax. It's as I suspected. Wires, wires, everywhere. I push on, following the contour of the eye socket.

Conducting fluid, cold and oozing, wets my fingers. In the back of my mind, I wonder where the real James has gone.

4

21.6.17

Yvonne Deering

For Rod

seeing clearly
you chose the solstice
for freedom

the longest night
then wintering
in the bardo

loved ones gather
(you were the eldest)
sacrificing an afternoon

eating and drinking
remembering
making music

while I in silence
ponder a poem
bleak as midwinter

I was the youngest
you tried to guide me
sometimes chided

as I listened
sometimes contended
you are not God

but you had journeyed
you had sat
beneath the Bodhi tree

and each new year
you gave me a moon chart
a guide to grow

your own work was good
your garden flowered
was fruitful

but it is done now
your journey over
your harvest in

now forty-nine days
from the solstice
you are the youngest

& seeing more clearly
from sunrise to sunset
I seek you

5

The Pine Cone on the Roof

Ben Downes

I was his gardener for years, but I didn't cut a single blade of grass.

It all started with a call. I listened to his calm voice and his requirements. I assumed I could accomplish all he wanted if I visited every three weeks. He sounded nice but assertive.

His name was Paul. He had slick blonde hair, wore black skinny jeans, a light-grey vest and Dunlop volleys.

On my first visit, he had me pruning his lemon tree, mowing his lawn and weeding a bed of irises. He'd tell me outlandish stories about previous workers he'd had and things that he'd gotten up to. They'd keep me entertained as I toiled away.

He'd had many gardeners before me, he said, and his reasons for dismissing them were various. One guy would sit out in the middle of the lawn and pray to some god of his. Buddhist or something. He didn't say exactly. Another just stopped turning up after a while. People were unreliable, Paul said. *I* was different.

I'd gotten to know his neighbour across the road. He was double Paul's age and called Red. Red knew a bullshit artist when he saw one. I liked Red; he was direct, and he hired me to look after his roses.

Paul liked Red, he said. He liked racing him out to the emptied garbage bins just to prove that even though he was younger he woke up earlier and was the better person because of it. Paul wasn't jealous that I was Red's gardener as well. He embraced it.

It's five years to the day since I finished working for Paul. I still have fond memories of working in his garden, raking up liquidambar leaves in autumn, mowing his buffalo grass, smelling the freshly cut lawn. It feels like yesterday.

I look over the road when I work at Red's and wonder what happened at Paul's. His garden is overgrown now—as if it has never been touched. The grass is high, the trees wild. I've never seen Paul come out and neither has Red. We know he's there. Or has been.

Red would tell me how Paul was different. Strange, even. Paul had issues. If he wasn't sick he had accidents. If he wasn't having accidents he'd be between jobs. I never knew what was real. He'd call his wife by other names and reminisce about jobs he once had, Red told me. Pigeon-breeder. Apiarist. Spy. Costume designer to the stars. Shoemaker. Everything about his life was weird.

Paul once put a pine cone on the top of my truck's cabin and told me that if something ever happened to him I could smell and touch the cone and they would be the things that I'd need to do to remember him by.

I was up my long ladder and about to trim a hedge at Red's when it occurred to me. I couldn't remember exactly when I worked for Paul. Whether it was summer or winter or a Monday or a Wednesday. And how many hours I did for him.

I forgot what Paul looked like. When I tried to remember his face, his eyes merged with his nose and then his cheekbones. In my mind, his mouth was a narrow endless tunnel into which I might tumble if I wasn't careful.

As I left Red's one day, I opened my glove box and came across a pine cone. I looked across the road as the wind picked up. The liquidambar that used to stand so handsomely in Paul's front garden was limp and frail. It hadn't had leaves for years.

6

Semi-Detached

Jane Downing

Declan doesn't remember the time before we moved to the suburbs. He doesn't believe there was a time when we were whole. He tells me to shut-up about the-time-before when I try to reminisce, like I've stolen something off him. He can't even remember the day our Dad drove the Cortina into our new driveway in Ballinclea Heights with a jovial left-right yank of the steering wheel to crunch the gravel better. He thinks my remembering there was another car in the adjacent driveway is far too obvious. 'A black Cortina to our white one, really?'

But it is true. As I was unbuckling the Declan of the time, a toddler too young for memories, from his booster seat, Mum said, 'look, the opposite of us.'

Her exclamation was a brief distraction from both our new home and our old one. We'd lost a cottage in a field, a daffodil meadow, and a rill running beside the lane, for this. Blank-eyed windows stared out at us, two up, two down. And ours was only half the house—we could only lay claim to the windows on our side of the shared wall. The two halves of the semi-detached presented a mirror image to the other, with the front door set at the furthest points, next to the garages for our opposite black and white cars.

As I hoisted Declan out of the Cortina onto my hip, jutting my pre-adolescent skinniness skilfully to provide a shelf for him to perch upon, a family spilled out from the opposite side of the semi-detached that was not ours. A father first dangling car keys, and a mother who clearly carried the shipwrecked Spanish genes of the west coast. The toddler on her hand negotiated the two steps from the door down to the garden path with as much concentration as a rock climber on the Dalkey Quarry wall. 'Careful,

Betty,' the mother cooed superfluously. Last came a shadow, a boy who, it transpired, was exactly my age.

Transpired, a word we both learnt at school the coming term along with transfer and transit. And he, the boy, privately taught me the thrilling extra, transubstantiation, because they were Catholic to our pious atheism.

The mother held up her free hand to wave and my bottle-blonde mother tilted her Jacky Onassis dark glasses from her nose as a return greeting.

'My sainted aunt,' my mother breathed so only I could hear, and Declan if only he could remember it, 'they really are the opposite of us.'

Declan says I am semi-deranged. No doubt others would argue there is nothing semi about either his or my derangement. But I try not to roll my eyes and get competitive about relative states of mental disturbance or grace. We, Declan and I, like to think we've put aside childish things like sibling rivalry.

Declan starts to have memories now to add to the narrative of our new life in the big city. Well, we thought of Dublin as a big city anyway. His early memories on our side of the duplex—a word he's brought back from America—are so bright with fun it is difficult to stare at them full in the face. We'd need Mum's knock-off haute couture shades.

'But you will agree we were the opposite of them?' I challenge him from the dizzying heights of adulthood.

'You always took things too literally,' he diagnoses.

'But all those times I walked in on you and Betty on our bedroom, wearing each other's clothes. You in those rainbow-coloured puckered tops—what were they called?'

'It's called smocking.' Declan was always able to provide the feminine details.

'And you'd borrow Mum's Woolworth's jewellery and dark glasses and in her high heels you'd dance and Betty'd pretend to be Fred Astaire.'

'Mick Jagger, I think,' he corrected.

I'd let him use my lipstick when he wore Betty's dresses. Crimson or experimental black, plus my nail polish in a choice of colours across the spectrum, because that sort of borrowing would be noticed by our mum if he pilfered from her stock. Declan was a beautiful child. He calls himself Erin now. I have trouble remembering that.

'And Betty was such a tomboy,' I remind him. Erin. Her. 'See, the opposites. All of us were the opposite of their family.'

'She was not and is not a tomboy,' Erin protests. 'Betty is now a perfectly ordinary woman with two perfectly ordinary children of her own.'

'You've kept in touch?'

She won't let me have my theory unchallenged. 'You pick and choose from our history to draw the right picture, to fit your ideas,' she accuses.

She will not accept that the facts built the theory in the first place.

I lay it all out. For my psychiatrist, my procession of lovers, for the detached part of myself who pretends normality. I enumerate the many ways in which we lived our lives in opposition. The cars; the toddlers growing into boys and girls, or girls and tomboys; the colour of our hair. War and Peace.

My parents fought. All the time. Every evening after we moved into the semi-detached, our dad came back intent on a row. He dumped his middle-management briefcase in front of the television, the thunder on his face sparking lightening in our bored and resentful mother. Declan and I kept our heads down and turned *Batman* up. But through the wall we heard no answering echo of strife. The mirror image through the shared wall was ass-about, reversed like any reflection. Uncle Ted and Aunty Dymphna, as we learnt to call them, got on. Sometimes even, when I lay in bed, I'd hear them laughing. Upstairs. Not downstairs in front of their television. Just them, alone in their bedroom.

The signs really were everywhere. I could see it even then, all the new pointers to my inevitable conclusion. One deep winter, nasty men came to take our car away because of something Dad did or did not have called credit. Credibility, credulity, credence: my opposite Sean and I shouted 'c' words at each other as we walked home from school in the crepuscular light. In the midst of which Sean told me their new Renault had just arrived because his da had been promoted to supervisor of all the restoration stonecutters at Dublin Castle.

I would never have questioned my home life if we'd stayed in the cottage, a whole family, surrounded on all sides by Nature. Repo men and brawling were just something that happened. The realisation that this was not so was bad enough. Then I realised the opposites between our families were not fixed. They sat on a balance.

Sean and I ran away one evening and sat on either side of the seesaw in the National School playground. Up he went to my thump down, the sound like Dad's flat hand on Mum's cheek. I was sad, he was happy. Full marks on the spelling test did that to anyone. Then to my surprise, and joy, I got all the spelling words right the following week and Sean was bullied by Fergal Dalton. Up my side of the seesaw soared, down plummeted Sean. My brother Declan, of the lovely countenance, lost his second front tooth leaving a whistling gap the very week both Betty's were revealed to have grown back perfectly. She smiled so prettily in the school photograph and Declan looked a thin-lipped grump.

I can go on. That is what I say to anyone who will listen. Then I usually do: with more examples, more data that could fit my theory and only my theory about them being the opposite of us.

On the rare hot days, when the temperature climbed above 18°C, my mother put on a white bikini and sat in the backyard on a banana lounge that didn't look a bit like any fruit we got down at Powers.' But Sean and Betty's mother vacuumed and sat indoors. Indeed, one sunny day she started knitting a new jumper for Sean who'd 'have grown out of everything he owns come winter, the rate he's going.'

See: opposites.

Our mum might have owned the bikini, but it was Aunty Dymphna who took us to the beach.

Killiney Beach was heaving with heat refugees on the *third* day of soaring temperatures if you can credit it! We squeezed in the back of their car not needing seatbelts we were so tight across the bench seat: Sean and me, Betty and Declan; the mums dark-haired and platinum blond, up front. Our mum smoking, ashing her cigarette out the window so it blew in on Declan and we all laughed.

By this stage Sean and I were confused teenagers. Our friendship was awkward, slipping between easy familiarity and startling moments of 'what is this man I see before me?' His thick, curly hair flopped over his eyes and he peered out a stranger. From his Marc Bolan hair to the T. Rex grunting when his voice broke mid-sentence, he was an enigma. No wonder I fell into quoting our school books to cover my clumsiness in the face of this new turn of events. 'Be still my beating heart,' I admonished myself, though it was more often a more clandestine part of the anatomy needing a talking to.

I suppose, looking back, Sean was feeling an equal and opposite hormonal rip beneath our intimacy. He never said in the time he was caught between a dinosaur obsession and the songs of the latest rock group. We were together, we were apart. We shot out of the Renault in our modest swimming costumes that day when we arrived at Killiney Beach. We hobbled barefoot over tarmac then pebbles until finally onto the beach proper, the sand burning our soles.

Declan and Betty threw a beach ball between them. In my memory they are a still-life, a happy snap, a painting titled The Last Carefree Moment, as Sean and I swept past into the shock of the water.

The water was cold of course. Sean shouted 'shit.' Not loud enough for the mothers to hear. We giggled at the wickedness words could accommodate.

It was best to keep on running, to brave the nipple-raising temperature, surging forward until our feet couldn't touch the ground. We circled with our legs kicking like we were riding bicycles under the sea and our arms breast-stroking like we might almost go somewhere, as we trod water and called out all the naughty words underlined by some sinner, who'd end up in Mountjoy prison for sure, in the class dictionary.

'Arse. Bitch. Crap. Damn. Fuck.'

Our legs touched underwater through no fault of mine. Or his. The shock was greater than you could get from some sparking electric eel swimming too close. He turned away from it. From me.

'Look how far I can swim,' he shouted back.

I can't keep up. I try. I can't. He's out against the blue sky. I scream that he wins, I lose, the law of opposites holding up again. I turned back to shore as he swam on.

Unsurprisingly, it was my parents who stayed together until death did them part. Despite his gambling and his debts and her amateur attempts at alcoholism. Unsurprising because I knew they would stay together the minute Aunty Dymphna walked out on Uncle Ted. There was no shouting, no fighting, no recriminations. One morning, Sean's ma was simply gone. And who can blame her, suffering as they were under such a weight of grief.

One psychologist said I am detached from reality. She did not laugh when I replied, 'only semi-detached.' So how would she understand the truth?

Declan tries but he is having his real life in America. He came back once as Erin to visit. She is a vision of loveliness. She misinterpreted my crying.

It was not that Erin had killed my little brother: it was that my new sister looked so much like our mother. Mum held my shivering body tight in a towel that day on the beach. I buried myself in her smells, her sweat and cigarettes and Charlie perfume, and she buried my ears in her embrace so I couldn't hear the shouting and the sirens.

Erin insisted during our last call in ascribing no masculine attributes to Betty. Betty is not a tomboy. Betty is ordinary. And maybe that is the balance of opposites for them: sat against his/her own *extra*ordinary presence.

And the balance for Sean and I is clear to me.

The breeze at the top of the Martello tower is soft. There's no-one else here, no-one to hear me argue the point. I threw my smart phone off the old fortification when Erin said again, 'it was not your fault.' She is like the rest of them. They want me to give up what they call my guilt.

The device shattered on the tower's foundation rocks below.

She knew I wasn't here to talk about my mental health. If she'd really listened she would truly understand I have no worries about myself on that score. They, the others, are so serious. So concerned about suicide. Why can't they see the miracle this is?

I am simply here to prove my theory.

There's no-one else on the tower, and there's no-one else on Dalkey Island today. Which is a pity: there's a lovely view. I can see across to the mainland. The beaches sparkle against the dark Irish Sea.

I can see the spot where Sean's body was landed after the search. I was not allowed see his body. I was not allowed go to the funeral. I was a child. Children didn't back then.

But I know for sure that because he died that day, I can live forever.

No-one believes me. But they were the opposite of us. And they remain the opposite of us.

7

The Revival of Miss Sally Parker

Natalie Evans

Now that she was older, it was clear to Sally that her neighbourhood was strange. As a child, she perhaps felt the feeling as one does a breeze, but it soon passed. Only now it niggled at her as she lay in bed at night and heard the wind flutter through the trees. Those were the times when she got to thinking. The unease burrowed like a worm into her stomach. Everyone walked in a jerky, mechanical motion and their limbs seemed strangely stiff. The same Cheshire-cat smiles spread across their shiny faces. The mothers had always been mothers, and the babies they pushed in prams never seemed to grow up. Every once in a while a new family moved in— but they too walked with sticky limbs and had sparkling clean faces.

Once or twice Sally had tried raising it with her parents, at the dinner table.

'Isn't Beatie getting too old for a pram now, isn't she seven or eight?'

'Sally! Beatrice is just a baby! Of course she should be in a pram.'

'Yes, yes I know.' Then Sally would bite her lip. 'I don't know, sometimes it feels like Beatie has been in that pram forever.'

Then she would stab at her potato and her father would reach for the gravy and life would go on.

'But when you saw Mrs Habernathy, don't you think she walks funny?'

'Funny?' said her father, sawing a roast carrot. 'How so?'

'That strange stop-start walk, her face, always so shiny but she's not sweating.'

'But Mrs Habernathy walks just the same as you or I dear,' said her mother.

Sally would shrug and take a sip of water and listen to her mother and father talking about the garden or the car or the weather instead.

At school Sally walked about with Millicent and noticed Mrs Habernathy across the street, and that's when she saw something she had never, ever seen before. Something descended from the sky. She couldn't make it out at first, and Millicent couldn't see it at all.

An enormous hand had materialised and grabbed a motionless Mrs Habernathy. It fiddled with something that projected from her back. Once Mrs Habernathy was placed upon the ground again she continued walking in her fast, spasmodic way, almost as if she were clockwork.

Then the hand did the same to Millicent, who had stopped dead. It was winding her up and upon her feet reaching the ground she trundled off again.

Then the hand picked up Sally, and she felt something twist in her back. Her feet back on the ground, she felt her arms and legs convulse. She was walking.

What she had grasped at all her life suddenly became clear. The truth appeared, and she tried to cry, realising that she couldn't change the fixed, plastic smile on her face.

8

Rumpelstiltskin

Louise Falconer

Cooper put his money on the counter and collected his not-skinny, not-soy, not-in-a-KeepCup flat white. He pushed his earbuds further into his ears and turned up the volume on his phone.

Cooper never had much to say and avoided unsolicited eye contact where he could. He was blessed with an inconspicuous appearance, which he capitalised on by dressing in jeans from Jeans West and t-shirts from Cotton On. He tended to attract women who found good-looking men intimidating.

Sipping on his coffee, Cooper pulled open the café door and turned into the town's pedestrian mall. It was a ten-minute walk from his small flat to the café, then through the mall to his office where he worked in payments. He had walked it five days a week, twice a day since graduating from TAFE five years before.

Like everyone in the town, Cooper knew the history of the mall. But unlike most people, it didn't trouble him. The mall perfectly suited the town.

A decade ago, the town's aldermen had issued a clarion call, demanding that the place realise its full potential and become 'the second most liveable regional, inland city.' There had been many committee meetings, and before the decade was even out, town planners mostly agreed that the desolate mall would be at the heart of their regeneration efforts.

An unprecedented level of activity from locals working for the dole meant the rejuvenated mall was ready for its opening before constituents' protests could gather traction. The mayor made a speech even longer than the ribbons he cut, and the secondary college band played 'Whiter Shade of Pale,' as they always did.

Bloated on their own hyperbole, media releases articulated carefully the benefits of this transformation. Of course, it was the left-wing press that noted how decades of neglect had irreversibly wormed their way into the texture of the buildings and flagstones. How, although freshly painted, the shopfronts retained their forlorn displays (checked shirts, orthopaedic shoes, mobility aids) and the pergola at the mall's centre still creaked under the weight of rampant ivy. The bins still permanently overflowed with Subway and McDonald wrappers, and birds continued to peck apathetically at discarded gherkins and jalapenos.

Cooper had no reason to think this day's walk through the mall would be different from that of any other. Yet, as Cooper passed by Best and Less, the music pumping through his earbuds stopped. A moment later, it was replaced by very loud, white noise.

'What the...?' Cooper pulled the lead from his phone. He turned the volume down and tentatively reconnected it. Silence. Sighing, he turned off the phone. While he waited for it to power up again he glanced around, chewing one of his fingernails.

At this time of day, the mall was always empty and, apart from the occasional squall of hungry birds, usually silent.

So, when Cooper heard what sounded like a flute, he involuntarily frowned. He shoved his earbuds in his jacket pocket and held his breath. It was most definitely a flute or—what was that thing he'd learned about in music classes—pan pipes? Something like that.

He started breathing again but remained still and listened. He tried to guess the direction of the music but it seemed like it was everywhere, all at once. He felt slightly uneasy that it was getting louder.

Though he hadn't been there moments before, it seemed completely natural that a small man was now sitting on a bench under the pergola a few metres away.

'Hello Cooper,' he said.

The man could be described only as compact. He was the size of an eight-year-old child, with small facial features and a long but tidy beard. He sat in a pin-striped suit with legs crossed and hands resting in his lap.

'Hello,' said Cooper.

'Come sit with me.' The man patted the wooden bench. Cooper hesitated.

'Do I know you?' he asked.

'Let's just say,' the man said with a small smile, 'that you don't *not* know me.'

'Oh.' Cooper sat down.

'Cooper. You work in an office not far from here, don't you?'

'Yes.'

'You don't enjoy your work particularly, do you?'

'S'okay.'

'Cooper,' the man's voice soothed, 'I know that you don't enjoy your work. I know that just on Saturday night you said to your friend Liam that you'd do anything to have a different job. Did you not?'

Cooper looked at his hands. He had been at the Commercial Hotel with Liam on Saturday night, but he couldn't remember anyone listening to their conversation.

'Were you there?' Cooper was sure that he'd recognise this man if he'd been at the pub; it was always the same crowd on a Saturday night.

'Let's just say that I wasn't *not* there.'

Cooper squeezed his eyes shut and opened them again. The little man was still there, smiling agreeably.

'Cooper. If I said that I could get you another job, with better pay and big bonuses—just like that,' the man snapped his fingers, 'what would you say?'

'Um... I'd say... Thank you?'

'Ahh, your mammy taught you well, Cooper.' He chuckled. 'You know, I can Cooper. I can have you walking into a new job this morning. A job that would pay you a six-figure salary. A job where *you* called the shots.'

In that moment, Cooper could see it all. The lift doors opening and him stepping out into the office, an expensive Italian suit jacket draped over his shoulder. He'd say good morning to his staff, they'd smile warmly at him from their desks. He'd stride across to his office; the sign on the door declaring in capital letters COOPER BRIGHT, M.D. His executive assistant would tentatively knock and ask about his coffee preferences. This morning he'd request a sausage roll from the bakery to go with his flat white. He'd sink into his leather chair and swivel to face the window. He'd have an unobstructed view of the mall.

The small man was talking again.

'Cooper. I can give you all this, but I need something from you. Not much of course, just a wee token of your gratitude. Cooper, would you be willing to exchange a wee token of gratitude for this opportunity?'

'I guess so...'

'You're a smart man Cooper. Let's see… How's about when you eventually select a beautiful bride from the crowds of women jostling for your love, you let me have a wee word with her on your wedding night. Just a wee word, maybe ten minutes or so. And then you and I will chat to see if there's anything else I can do for you. You know that there will *always* be more I can do for you.'

Cooper thought about this for a moment. It seemed reasonable.

'It is very reasonable.' The man grinned. 'I want to tell you Cooper, I don't do this for just anyone. I've picked you specially.'

Cooper was about to ask the man why. Why had he been chosen? But he paused.

He cast his mind back to the conversation with Liam on Saturday night. They were at the pub celebrating because Liam had a new job with one of the town's lawyers.

'Mate,' Liam had said, 'I think I've hit the big time.' Cooper laughed.

'No, I'm serious mate. The main lawyer, he does conveyancing mostly, but he said he sometimes goes over to the courthouse. Has to stand in front of the judge and all that. He said that I could go with him to see what it's like.'

'Well, it'll be a change visiting court with Mr Pole-Up-His-Pants than with your old man, I guess.'

Liam ignored Cooper's comment and pressed on. 'But how cool is that? You've got to admit Coops, it is pretty cool. Me working in a law firm. Who knows where it could lead?'

'Mate. I really don't want to burst your bubble, but you've got a job as some kind of beaver creature working for a shitty small-town lawyer.'

'I'm a "go-for", not a gopher,' Liam had said quietly, looking down at his beer. 'Coops, don't be an arsehole. This is my chance. I need to make the most of it. What bloody else is there?'

The truth of it thudded hard into Cooper's chest. Liam's words hung in the air and Cooper felt ashamed.

Every year since they'd met, Liam and Cooper had conspired about how they would escape the town. At fourteen, they'd swaggered about the skate park, bemoaning their boredom, imagining the girls lying in wait for them in the city. At twenty, as they careered around the town's three roundabouts in Liam's Corolla, P-plates abandoned, pissed as newts, they swore blind that they would not be—*not be*—stranded in this shit-hole. They would find a way out, make themselves rich and never, ever look back.

'What bloody else is there?'

In that moment, Cooper grasped how keenly Liam was clinging to his scrap of opportunity and felt only pity. It surprised him that Liam had not yet accepted what Cooper had reconciled himself to years before: they were never leaving this town. It had defeated them. Men like them didn't go places, they didn't strike it rich. They shagged the local hairdressers, spawned new life unexpectantly, and before they realised, found themselves mortgagors of a three-beddie with rising damp on a street that was built too narrowly for garbage trucks.

'You're totally right mate. I'm sorry.' Cooper drained the froth at the bottom of his glass. 'I reckon I'm just jealous. I'd give anything for a new job, let alone a job like that. Tell you what though, you'll be shouting the beers once you're a hotshot lawyer.'

Liam smiled broadly. 'Too right. Reckon I'll shout you one now so I can get used to how it feels.' Liam stumbled to the bar, high-fiving the barman they'd known since year nine. They'd had a big night, both of them drinking and drinking, stalwart in their ambition to forget.

As Cooper stood in the pedestrian mall, he realised he wasn't interested in knowing why this little old man had singled him out. He wasn't interested in hearing anything at all from him. It was far too late.

The man sensed the shift in Cooper's thinking.

'Cooper? Are you still with me on this one? A new job! Think of it—the envy of your friends. Women suddenly desperate for your attention.'

Unbidden, the scene flared in Cooper's mind again: the lift doors opening, his stepping out into the office, an expensive Italian suit draped around his shoulders. He'd say good morning to his staff…

'No,' Cooper said, and the images flickered then dissolved.

The little man leaped from the seat to his feet, his eyes now parallel with Cooper's navel. 'What do you mean "no"?'

'Dunno,' said Cooper, 'Just don't think it's for me.'

The man stamped his foot, his body sparking with anger. 'I cannot believe,' he spat, 'you are telling me this.'

Cooper's brows furrowed. 'I'm sorry… uh… sir. It just seems like a lot of hassle, you know? I mean, my job right now isn't great. But y'know, I can just do my thing and go home. Go to the pub if I want to. Watch telly of an evening. If I was, like, managing people and projects and stuff, I'd have to, you know…'

'Stuff? Cooper…! I cannot believe I have wasted my time with you.'

Cooper chewed his lip. 'Like I said, I'm really sorry. I just can't see the point.'

The man's eyes swivelled in their sockets. 'Can't see the point? Do you know how many men would kill, and I mean literally kill for this chance?' Spittle flew from his mouth, landing unceremoniously in his beard. 'Is it because you're worried about the arrangement, about the wedding night? Is that it? I can tell you now boy, that arrangement…'

Somewhat out of character, Cooper interrupted. 'It's not really anything to do with that actually.'

'God forfend!' The man started hopping from left foot to right, his hands curled into tight fists.

Cooper stifled a yawn and checked the time on his phone. 'Sorry, mate, but I really need to go. I've got to be at work in five.'

'May your friends and fortune forsake you!' the man shrieked. 'May the earth open up and swallow you whole.'

'Ah… okay,' Cooper said, 'Maybe see you around?'

'May a falcon peck out your right eyeball. May you fall into an unattended mineshaft and break every vertebra.' The man continued to stamp his feet, his small face purple with rage.

Cooper took his earbuds from his pocket and pushed them into his ears. He pressed play on his phone. He turned to wave to the little man, but he was no longer there—two pigeons paced about where he'd been standing. One was pecking at a gap in the flagstones trying to rescue a french fry, becoming agitated by the lack of quarry. The other bird stared unblinkingly at Cooper. Its throat pulsed gently. Cooper shrugged and began walking towards the end of the mall.

9

The Darkest Pit in Me

Travis Franks

I might be addicted to sadness.
Perhaps, like many 'glitches' we detect in ourselves as adults, my maudlin obsession began in childhood. I can only assume our teacher mistakenly showed us *Watership Down*, because no eight-year-old is psychologically equipped for that cinematic experience. But it was as pivotal as it was harrowing. It left a dark mass on my subconscious. Art Garfunkel's *Bright Eyes* reverberated through the subsequent years. I was haunted by abstract images of tormented rabbits. Equal parts terrified, devastated and enamoured by these stimuli, I kept picking at these memories as though they were scabs. Scratching at wounds to see what I bled. It ached every time, but the sorrow was satisfying.

I feel inspired after being traumatised.
Jonathan Safran Foer's (father) figure falling from the World Trade Centre. I turned to my notebook. Reading *The Lovely Bones*, I paused to write a poem. The moment Susie Salmon's soul 'shrieked out of earth' and reached out for one last human connection. This duende leaves me with a hollowed-out feeling I fill with words. I grapple the ache, resisting its fleeting nature as though it's an uncooperative cat I desperately want to love me. I repurpose the pain, make it my own.

I write under the influence of music.
Eerie and emotive, the kind that sweeps me up and plunges me down into shrouded places swirling with echoes. I want to *feel* what I write. Music is a powerful catalyst, it floats feelings up to the surface, but you can't control what's dredged from the depths.

I emulate slippery machinations of melancholy in my written worlds.

In *Presque Vu*, a boy undergoing psychotherapy is on the verge of recovering a repressed trauma… but not quite. In *Swansong*, the relationship between a clinically depressed mother and her queer pre-adolescent son is further strained by witnessing the fall of a circus performer. In *The Blue Hour*, I lament the loss of a childhood friend to long distance and drug addiction. In my pursuit of the bittersweet ever after, the poem ends:

> These days, I write your name on blank pages
> And wait for you to reappear.

I dip my pen in the inkwell of bruises.

In *Why I Write*, Joan Didion speaks of being compelled by the things that 'shimmer.' What if I'm not drawn to a shimmering? What if I'm attracted to shadows? And I come to wonder if my preoccupation with melancholy—if the shadows—conceal something specific. If I'm perpetually wading through childhood jetsam. Writing: a dressing of wounds. A controlled bleeding. A 'literary leeching.' Writing in circles around a black hole. Writing myself *into* a black hole. How do I get out again if I get in over my head?

In my early twenties I would pass out on my friend's couch while watching the music clip to Bjork's *Pagan Poetry* on repeat. Her lyrics tell of a relationship she knows is doing her damage, but to which she is inexorably drawn.

And I think, 'that's me and melancholy.'

> Pedalling through the dark currents, I find
> An accurate copy
> A blueprint of the pleasure in me

References

Sebold, Alice. *The Lovely Bones*. Picador Classic, 2015.

Bjork. 'Pagan Poetry.' *Vespertine*. One Little Indian, 2001.

10

The Uninvited Guest

Catherine Gillard

When she heard her husband's car she stopped chopping the wood and watched him drive up the long, unsealed driveway. The car crunched to a stop in the gravel. She placed a piece of jarrah on the block, raised the axe and brought it down, sending the two halves flying. Keith had been threatening to buy one of those new gas heaters, the pretend ones, with the fake flame that was only a flickering coloured ribbon. Better for the environment, he'd said. And you won't have to nag me to chop the wood.

That's why she'd started doing it herself. He was not getting rid of her pot belly stove. There had been other shifts in the demarcation between *his* jobs and *her* jobs since he'd retired and she'd had her operation. Without any discussion, it was she who now killed the chook for Sunday roast.

After a vague wave of his hand, Keith silently unloaded pot plants from the boot and ferried them to the veranda: a struggling miniature rose bush in a chipped terracotta pot, a silver lady fern with curled brown leaves, a drooping kentia palm and her least favourite, the common old Dieffenbachia, otherwise known as a dumb cane. Did he have no idea that the sap was caustic and that gloves were required for handling that one? He'd not said a word about the nursery before he left. Perhaps because she might have insisted on coming. Not plants she'd have chosen, especially not the ugly Dieffenbachia, but she kept that to herself. It was years since he'd come home bearing gifts.

He fetched a painting from the back seat, not at all to her taste either, all bright modern geometric shapes in acrylic. Their walls were already crowded with her landscapes and watercolours from art class and photos of their daughter and grandchildren.

'Where's that going?' she asked, her tone suggesting the garage, if not the burn-off pile.

'Wherever you like,' he said and carried it inside. Next he took in three cardboard boxes.

She guessed now he'd been to a garage sale but asked anyway, 'Where on earth have you been?' They were due for their own cleansing purge, not more junk from other peoples' weekend chuck outs.

He blinked a few times, the give-away sign he'd heard her but was unwilling to answer. When he lifted out the animal carrier from the passenger seat and she glimpsed the dark thing inside, she was too shocked to repeat the question. He avoided her eyes as he walked passed, his sinewy arms bulging. She rushed after him, forgetting she was still clutching the axe.

'Shut the door!' he commanded when they were both inside.

She reflexively obeyed. 'You can't bring that here, you know—'

His eyes widened and she realised she had raised the axe. She lowered it and leant it against the wall.

'I'm doing someone a favour.'

The inside of her nose tickled unpleasantly. 'And the plants?' she gestured outside.

'They were dying.'

Not a garage sale then. 'Take them all back to where they came from—'

'I can't.'

Her head throbbed dully. She touched her nose, her sinuses ached. He left the room and returned empty-handed.

'Where is it?' she asked.

'In Mary's room. She'll run away otherwise.'

She. She had suspected it was female, but she wouldn't ask its name. She rubbed her eyes, unable to soothe the itching. There was nothing irrational about her loathing. The allergy specialist had explained how their sebaceous glands oozed a sticky poison that glued to hairs and dust particles and produced a toxic fog inside the house. Even if she vacuumed, scrubbed and wiped from now until midnight, allergens would linger for months.

'You have to get rid of it.' She rubbed her temples in a circular motion. A tight band around her chest was shrinking. An invisible torturer prodded her eye sockets with hot pokers.

He put his hands to his back, arched and yawned.

'There's that animal rescue place in Busselton. Take it there.'

'She's not going into a cage.'

She retreated to the bedroom to swallow anti-histamines and a paracetamol and puff on her asthma spray, then she drew the curtains and lay down on top of the freshly-bleached white doona, still wearing her outdoor clothes. Slowly, the cocktail of medication released the tension in her jaw and eased the thudding in her temples. She recalled some snippet of fact about cats running away from strange places to seek familiar territory. And the trick of applying butter to their paws so that while they licked it off, they got used to new surroundings, and she supposed, associated the new place with the taste. She got up to hide the butter tub.

On the way back to bed she lingered in the passage just outside the spare room, their daughter's old bedroom. The door was ajar. Keith lay on his side on the single bed, his back to her, facing the open metal grate of the carrier. He murmured something before placing his hand inside and gently scooping out the thin black cat.

'Keith?'

He turned over and the cat jumped onto the ground and disappeared under the bed. Keith rose and it appeared again at his feet, circling his legs in figure eights, its tail flicking in agitation. She fled back to her room and waited for him to come to her with a proper explanation. She was still waiting into the evening, when habit propelled her into the kitchen to prepare dinner. The last of the sun's orange rays penetrated the glass doors, illuminating the agitated dust particles in the air. The TV droned with the nightly news. She peeled potatoes. Keith opened the fridge for a pre-dinner beer, poured her a wine without asking. 'You know what they do to me,' she said, gouging out a potato eye with the end of the peeler.

He cracked his can open. 'It's only temporary.'

'You wanting to kill me?'

He smiled, raised the beer to his lips and tilted back his head.

'When are they—' she coughed, wiped at her itchy eyes with the back of her hand—'coming back?'

'What?'

Years of working with farm machinery had wrecked his hearing but she suspected half the time he used his partial deafness as a pretence not to answer her.

'When are *they* coming back? For their cat?'

He avoided her eyes again. 'They've gone. For good.'

'So why did you get stuck with it?'

He shrugged. Adjusted his hearing aid, tuned her out.

It was not a big town, and though she was not sociable like Keith, had not been born here like him, she knew most of the locals. Had taught them, and some of their children too. The fabled tale of the green city teacher swept off her feet by the bachelor farm boy.

She could go to Mary's. For a couple of weeks. But she had only just returned from visiting her daughter in the city—a household in perpetual chaos—Mary practically a single mother with her husband away on the mines.

'I'll put her outside,' Keith said, 'but she's used to the run of the place.'

So was Margaret.

She wordlessly placed the soup and bread on the kitchen table.

'Are we out of butter?' he asked, shouting above the TV volume.

She could play deaf too.

The cat was shut out but Keith exiled himself to the back veranda as well and then carried the toxins back in on his clothes and skin. Sometimes during the day Margaret would stand at the window, sneezing and scratching herself, repulsed yet fixated on the drama of it chasing birds or stalking invisible prey. Its sleek black body was perfectly adapted for hunting and killing. It would freeze, coiled to pounce if the target came within striking distance. The chase never lasted long. Either it caught its quarry or gave up quickly, saving its energy for the next victim.

When she saw the cat staring at a bobtail, mouth open wide and blue tongue on display, she ran out to the back garden to save the lizard. But her intervention was too late. The bobtail was already a wriggling bloody stump impaled on a paw. While the cat's attention was fixed on its still twitching prize she uncoiled the garden hose, twisted the nozzle and turned on the tap. The hard jet of water sent it scarpering over the back fence and from then on it was even more wary of Margaret.

Most mornings she found the lifeless bodies of birds or mice on the back doorstep. She left them for Keith, who picked up the corpses with a plastic bag over his hand and dumped them in the wheelie bin. She imagined chopping the cat's head off with the axe like she did with the chickens and dumping it in too.

'That bell around its neck doesn't work,' she said.

'It's just her instinct. What we humans bred them to do. Kill rodents.'

'It kills for fun.'

'Your fault.'

'Me?' she asked, squeezing the inhaler case in her apron pocket.

'She can't hunt if she's inside.'

Keith started bringing the cat in at night, at first shutting it in the laundry but before long the creature was strutting around Margaret's home as if it owned it. The itching progressed to a rash on her jaw that slowly spread down her neck. When she queried him about the rehoming arrangements, he would tell her there were a few people who might be interested.

When Keith left for his audiology appointment she searched the garage for the cat carrier but couldn't find it. She tipped out the contents of one of the boxes Keith had brought home with the cat. She had forgotten about them, but now she studied the eclectic assortment of books: cookbooks, mysteries, thrillers and several sports biographies. She clawed at the rash that had now spread to her chest.

Wearing her gardening gloves, she carried the box into the back yard. 'Here Kitty!' she said, trying to sound inviting, but her voice came out wheezy and the cat jumped off the swinging chair and fled beneath it. She kneeled down and saw it had flattened itself against the brick wall of the house. Its witchy eyes glowed yellow. She grabbed at it but the cat hissed and flipped onto its back. Her gloves offered no protection and its claws sliced heat into her skin. She breathed in quick puffs, feeling the rising panic of an asthma attack. Gritting her teeth, she grabbed for the collar and hauled it out. She held it up, elongated, squirming and choking as its collar bore its full body weight. She dumped it into the box and quickly folded down the flaps, sealing the box with masking tape.

Her throat constricting, she swallowed with difficulty. She grabbed her inhaler from her cardigan pocket, wrapped her shaking hands around it, pressed and breathed in the vapour as deeply as she could. Once she felt calmer, she carried the box to her car, depositing it onto the back seat. She reversed down the driveway, thumping over a few potholes. It scratched against its cardboard tomb, but she drowned out the sound with the radio. After the Mahler symphony, a news reader announced the death of a twenty-nine-year-old woman and a thirty-five-year-old man in a head-on collision with another vehicle on a notorious single lane highway in the State's far north, finishing with the road toll for the holiday period and comparing the number of fatalities in Western Australia with the other States.

Did other countries keep a running tally of road deaths for the public? Or was it only in Australia that the states ran this macabre competition. And the winner with the worst drivers goes to…

She drove along the same stretch of Bussell Highway she'd seen on the TV a few weeks earlier reporting another fatality, past a simple white wooden cross on the side of the road with an elaborate but wilting bunch of flowers. The cat yowled and scratched frantically until it gave up and fell silent.

She slowed down and swerved to the side of the road. Getting out of the car she looked up at the grey skies hanging low, about to collapse upon her. At her feet lay the detritus of civilization—fast food wrappers, iced-coffee and Coke bottles, straws—discoloured and disintegrating on the shallow shoulder of the road. She retrieved the cardboard box from the back seat and strode past a sentry of eucalypts lining the road, pushed through straggling bush into a paddock which was more shallow pond than pasture. A vapour rose thick from the earth as her feet sank into the soggy ground up to her calves. Silence but for the mud sucking at her wellington boots. Midgies, those tiny annoying little insects the size of a pin, swarmed but she couldn't swat them away while she clutched the box. Only the females bit, the blood a protein source for their eggs. That was common knowledge, but less well known was that they were hungrier around a full moon. And there it was, just over the horizon, full and milky, rising in the late-afternoon sky.

A one-legged raven regarded her warily as she approached, head cocked to one side, before returning its attention to the small furry dead animal under its claw, to peck and pluck at its innards. Her legs screamed with the effort of marching though the sludge. She tired easily since the operation six months ago, when she had given birth to her own womb. After discovering the malignant growth that had caused her to bleed heavily for days and days the surgeon had recommended removing her uterus, along with her ovaries, as a precautionary measure, a pre-emptive strike against the growing tumour.

She congratulated herself on avoiding being tripped by a partially submerged truck tyre only to fall over a minute later on a blackened tree branch, rising out of the wet earth like a serpent. The box flew from her hands. She looked up, tasting rotting earth. Frenzied scratching came from the box. As she stood up she considered turning around, leaving the cardboard coffin half-submerged in the muddy water. But she wiped the dirt from her eyes with the back of her hands, picked up the box and continued her heavy-footed march.

She reached more solid ground and trudged along a track worn into existence by a tractor or truck. The box grew heavier by the minute. Little grew here, the soil made infertile by the rising tableland, too much water, too much salt. Even the skeletal eucalypts refused to recolonise this wasteland. She stopped and shook the box, listened to the distressed mewling.

'Who did you belong to?' she whispered to the box. And the plants, the painting, the books. She acknowledged what she had been trying to hide from herself. A woman. Gone away. Or dead. Keith had brought his dead mistress' pitiful legacy into her home. She had blamed her husband's cool detachment, lack of purpose and bouts of drunkenness on post-retirement fug and depression, and her medical procedure that had cauterised all sexual desire for him. She saw now that it had been grief. The loss of a lover.

Staggering onwards, she recalled the day a few months earlier when her car, loaded with shopping, wouldn't start. Her call to Keith went to message bank. The second call was to the golf club. The manager said she hadn't seen Keith despite Margaret's insistence he was playing that afternoon. Her next call was to the tow truck company. Keith's explanation that evening had been vague but plausible. But there were other occasions when he'd told her he was playing golf—while his clubs sat idly in the garage.

A rumbling in the distance animated the box again. She squinted up at the bleak darkening sky. Ragged fast-moving clouds had shrouded the moon. Rain spat on her face. She dumped the box at last, ripped open the flaps and stepped back. The yellow eyes glared at her. The cat hissed, lips pared back.

'Scram!' she shouted. The cat leapt out of the box and ran, a shadow skimming across the muddy ground. Should she have taken it to the cat haven instead? It would have been kinder to the native animals. Or one quick chop with her axe. Too late now. The creature was gone. She turned and trudged back to the car, the rain settling into a steady drumming on her head.

She opened the car door and kicked off her wellie boots, slick with fetid mud. She turned on the heater and drove in her thick warm socks. Her wet clothes filled the car with an earthy rotting stench but already her lungs felt clearer, her head less woolly. She slowed down as she approached the white cross, wanting to read her name.

No. Not a woman's name. Peter.

At dinner Keith asked if she'd seen *her*. He was worried that she hadn't appeared for her tin of tuna. He thought she might be lost. Or worse.

She had put her inhaler back in the bathroom cabinet. Her rash had receded and her eyes and nose no longer streamed. But she couldn't clear her mind, wondering if the creature had fallen victim to feral cats, starvation, or two tonnes of fast-moving metal. Or was it still prowling the marsh at night? Sometimes she felt her scalp shrink. Sensed she was being watched. Followed. Then a black streak would pass across her vision.

At night dull yellow orbs floated in the darkness of her dreams. The creature jumped onto her bed and padded along her sleeping body. It kneaded her face with razor sharp claws, then licked the blood that oozed from her skin. She tasted fur and woke struggling for breath in a tangle of damp sheets. On his back, mouth slack, Keith snored the rumble of a giant purring feline. And somewhere outside, a tapping sound.

The next morning she discovered a half-dead rat, twitching in a sea of early morning dew, eyes glazing as life seeped away. She looked up to see Keith next to her, smiling. Late in the afternoon, the cat appeared at the glass sliding door, its legs barely holding up its scrawny body, its right eye milky with infection. She ignored the paws on the glass, *tap tap tap*, the weak mewling, until Keith wrapped it up in one of his coats and drove away. Margaret swallowed an anti-histamine and several strong pain killers she'd had left over from the hysterectomy, washed down with a few neat whiskies.

Keith returned well past dinner time carrying the cat, partly shaved and bandaged. Margaret's eyes streamed as she retrieved a suitcase from the top of the wardrobe. In slow motion she folded clothes and squeezed them in until the case was bulging. Keith watched her from the bedroom door. He sat on the bed, put his hands to his face and wept. She couldn't recall the last time she'd seen him cry. At Mary's birth? She stopped packing, sat next to him, placed an arm around him. He allowed himself to be comforted, his face against her breasts, soothed like a child. She kissed the top of his head, balding, pink and slightly scaly. At last he was coming back home. He sniffed deeply and wiped his eyes on her shirt, leaving behind those damp spots she'd had there when nursing Mary. She waited for the apology, acknowledgement of her injury, confession and repentance. She didn't trust herself to speak. She should lie down now, under the doona, gently pull him into an embrace, undress him, comfort him with her body. She was a taut string ready to vibrate at his touch. Her skin flushed, her lips parted to say his name.

'Margaret,' Keith said, swallowed, opened his mouth to speak, but something caught his eye. She followed his gaze. Keith disentangled himself from her and picked up the cat. Stroked it. The yellow eyes glared at her, triumphant.

'I've wasted years on you,' she said, quietly. 'Why didn't you leave me when I could have started again?' The memories of their life together curdled, like lemon added to milk.

She snatched more clothes from her dresser drawers. Yes, better she go and get Mary on her side first. Oh, there'd been an affair alright, of that she was certain. She zipped the suitcase shut and tugged it from the bed. Keith moved to help but she pushed past him and dragged it to the car. She didn't like the idea of being an uninvited house guest. She doubted Mary would like it either. But for now she didn't know what else to do, where else to go. Later maybe she'd book a berth on a cruise ship and sail the Mediterranean, on her own.

The sun sank through a tumult of red stained clouds, leaving the plum-evening sky. She stared at the house, unable to start the engine, imagining the cat curled up on Keith's lap, purring. She wound down the window and gulped in the cold night air. Fat drops of rain splattered onto the windscreen. She turned the ignition and threw the gear into reverse, but kept her foot on the brake as Keith ran towards her.

'The cat is all I have left.'

'Of her?' she said, showing him she *knew*.

'Of him.'

She released the brake and stomped on the accelerator. She repeated his words as she drove. Until they made no sense. Until they were just sounds. Of him. Of him. Of him. Off him. Off him. Off hymn. Off hymn. Ovum. Ovum.

The headlights swept through bullets of rain as she sped north along the highway, feeling the unbounded possibilities of driving fast, the wind fingering her loose hair. The ear worm buried deeper into her head: Of him. Of him. The cat's all I have left. Off hymn. Ov Vim. Ovum.

As she approached the little white cross on the side of the highway she slowed down to read the name again. Squinting through the rain and whisky. Peter. She accelerated away, her skin prickling with the sense of a presence behind her. The rear vision mirror showed only black empty road. She shortened her focus and stared at her face, eyes wild and round and red, hair dishevelled like a mad woman's. And the glowing yellow eyes.

Something tore at her head. She removed her hands from the wheel to protect her face. Shrieks vibrated in her eardrums. Her eyes burned as she tasted fur. She tumbled like dirty clothes in a washing machine, the seatbelt biting into her clavicle. Darkness. Pain in her shoulder. No feeling below that. The stench of burning rubber, petrol. The taste of thick blood, acrid smoke. A hissing sound, steam pissing from the bonnet. Rain drumming on the roof, on her skull.

After a time, in the distance, the klaxon of an ambulance. And then the red strobe illuminating the sleek black shadow dragging itself to the white cross.

11

Panning for Tink

Lauren Hay

'——atest in a string of small fires, lit in the east of the state, in the bathrooms of abandoned or condemned buildings. The local fire service has released a statement——'

Static interrupts the café radio as a ghastly squall howls outside, throwing leaves, litter and rain alike down the darkened street and against the café's windows.

'——ve advised the public these fires are unlikely to escalate. The starters of the fires, the authorities believe, are members of our homeless community looking to keep warm—in what has been a bitterly cold autumn.'

A young man—grown, but with the sort of face impossible to approximate an age for—snorts into his cup of sugary long black. He's seated in a booth, giving the impression that there isn't space in the empty seats for company. The man wipes his face, clearing it of too-sweet coffee spittle. The man's name is Julius.

His fingers trawl over his phone's filthy touchscreen. He's reading an article on a shadier part of the net and ignoring Peter's impatient messages pinging at the top of the screen. Julius knows the dealer will only be asking when the next batch of tink will be available. *Ping!* Julius sighs.

'In other news, police have been kept busy investigating the sixth person to go missing in as many weeks—this time a year-six student, Belinda Bird. Her parents are understandably distraught...'

As the reporter wraps up her account of the missing-persons story, citing Facebook pages and hotline numbers, Julius sighs and returns to his lukewarm drink—unpleasant but necessary to cleanse his palate. That the authorities aren't more concerned about the wackjob pyro who's been lighting up all over town is laughable, he thinks. Although, it's not like they have any real reason to suspect anything is awry, he supposes, eyeing the clock above the counter. Dave better be on time. Julius drains his cup, raises his hood and shells a pink note from his wallet, which he pushes into the tip jar as he exits the café. It's pay-day, after all.

Julius is meeting Dave at a motel. It's only a few blocks from the café, but in the gale outside—which strikes him, pulling and hounding his wiry limbs—Julius is soaked through in moments. Even bitterly cold, he smiles. Sliding a hand into a secret pocket in his jacket, he reaches for something familiar and comforting. An *etui*. The tube-like container—an antique needle-case, made of bone—once belonged to Julius's grandmother. Inside are not needles, but both the tool and product of Julius's family's trade: tink. It costs an arm and a leg, so for those with the ability to pan for tink, it's a very lucrative business. But one pays a hefty moral price to wield the magical element. Without the gene that triggers magic production in his cells, Julius and those like him must rely on harvesting the magical essence from other people. Known in the trade as *humines*, these people have been kept ignorant of their magical potential. It's Julius's job to sniff out tink-carriers from the general human populace. Tink-panners might not carry the gene that creates magic—but they do carry one that allows them to sense it.

He's also more proficient than most at using tink and subsequently uses less of his product; the reason for Peter's interest in his harvest. An interest Julius is rightly wary of. Julius may be Peter's best supplier but he surely isn't his only panner, Julius remembers.

Julius licks his lips. He eyes the motel's garish fluorescent sign and his smile becomes a grin. Once inside Julius crosses the room, ignoring the occupied reception staff, and proceeds directly to the men's toilets. He checks the stalls, all empty, and locks the door. Julius retrieves the *etui*, a musty notebook from his pockets and a second small tin box. He places the paraphernalia on the countertop and leafs through the notebook. He licks his lips, fingers tapping, flitting, dancing between the *etui* and the tin. They settle on the tin as his eyes dart around his grandmother's squiggly script.

- 1973

Morphing Spell - Garder:

To ensure the host doesn't reject the casting, the relevant humor of the phisiological aspect, must be introduced to the Ash; to convince it of its impending autonomy to the host.

— Jillian Bel.

Deftly, he loosens his jeans, a hand nudging the material to bare his skin. He pushes aside coarse hair to reveal the crease between his thigh and groin. Reflected in the bathroom vanity are a multitude of small, white scars—brandings of previous castings.

Julius takes some alcohol-swabs and a lancet from the tin box. He licks his lips and swabs the countertop. Then, lancet in hand, he presses the blade deep enough to tickle his lymph-nodes. Wincing, he smears the bloody blade across the sterilised section of counter. From the *etui* he pours a fine grey powder—fastidiously, meticulously—atop the smeared blood.

The powder makes a twinkling sound. *Tink. Tink. Tink.* Julius giggles. A breathy, whispered, secret glee. The powder blushes pink but takes on no damp quality—in fact, it appears to smoulder. He selects from his kit a thin cylinder and an atomiser no bigger than a finger. He uncaps the atomiser and, with haste, taps a miniscule amount of the powder from the etui into the bottle and caps it again. Exhale. Breathe. He pants. His hands are less steady now that the worst is over. Everything is in order. Julius aligns a nostril to an end of the cylinder, the other end to the powder. He breathes out then inhales.

Plink!

Dropping the tube, he rolls his face over the cool counter top, all smiles. He sniffs. Once at the familiarity of the feeling and once at the feel of tink in his nasal passages. His heart warms. As he sets about putting away his kit, he's careful to avoid looking in the mirror.

It's not long before Julius's chest feels heavy. The jeans he wears grow tight across his hips; his shoes feel too big. His hair, longer now, disrupts his vision. Despite his discomfort, Julius's good mood persists. He undoes the top two buttons of his shirt. He glances in the mirror at the reflection that isn't his own, but that he's seen often enough to begin to feel as if it is. Julius's face is softer, his eyes dark. He fastens his jeans, washes his hands and, clearing his slender throat, exits the bathroom.

Standing outside the men's-room's door is an employee, befuddled that it's locked. He's startled when a busty, wirily-limbed woman strolls through the door. Julius blinks at the bespectacled kid in the motel's bland uniform, winks and continues on his way. A carved, wooden clock hangs above the reception desk. Julius glances at it, eight on the dot, and bites his lip a moment. His thinner, arching brows come together in a frown. Dave better not be late; Julius loathes wasting tink. He grinds the toes of his too-big boots into the threadbare, crumb-full, vomit-patterned carpet and broods.

He smells Dave before he sees him. *Humines* have such sweet scents. Dave's scent isn't the only giveaway to his identity; he is young and has a bumbling attitude. Julius grins. He takes a moment to appreciate that Dave is a good head taller than he is before sauntering over and linking a thin, feminine arm through Dave's. Dave starts.

'Wha...'

'Dave, right?' Julius's voice is soft and husky. His eyes, bright and happy.

'Julie?'

'Gotcha.' Julius giggles.

'How'd... we've never met. How did you know?'

'Mmm.' Winking, Julius presses himself to Dave. 'I've got a nose for these sorta things.'

How Julius came by his identity isn't so much of a problem for Dave. He is distracted by Julius's warm, fleshy, feminine front.

'Oh. Oh—kay. You're. Um... very nice, ah.' Dave's words sputter with his breath. His pulse spikes. Julius rubs his fingers into the silky skin of Dave's inner bicep to feel the veins beneath. They throb. Pleased, Julius alters his own breathing to something deeper—knowing it will cause his bust to heave. He checks Dave's gaze to be sure and giggles quietly to see the man so ensnared by his tink-induced assets. Someone coughs; another customer, or perhaps the receptionist herself.

Julius sweetens his smile. 'How about some privacy. Would you like to get a room?'

There's a stupid look on Dave's face. 'Yeah... yes! I'll. One moment. I'll be right back.' Dave bumbles his way over to the receptionist.

'You better!' Julius calls with a playful wave of girlish fingers. Dress-up was never such fun!

Dave babbles on the way up to their room. *I've never done this before! With a... Like, a... I mean I've done* it *before but not... this!* Julius has heard it all before. He plays the role of doll-eyed sex worker like an obliging older sibling to a child's make-believe. Ah! He feels so hot. Not completely aroused—not yet. But a disquieting sort of anticipation. This is an emotional high, a power trip. Dave is something simple and innocent that he can toy with. His belly, hands and heart sear.

Dave gets grabby when the door to their room closes. His hands are on Julius's chest and arse and his tongue is in Julius's mouth. Julius's body throbs at the attention. Huge in his chest, his heart thumps, excited—terrified. His diaphragm judders as Dave slides hands beneath the soft cotton of his shirt. Despite knowing the seduction is a lie his vagina begins to ache pleasantly. His mind pulls away from the arousal but cannot quite leave it. Dave slides a hand to cup, pull—*pinch*—Julius's breasts. The arches of his feet tingle. Julius judders. Sighs. He relishes the throb of his clit for a moment. Two. Torn between euphoria and revulsion. A woman's body is a dangerous thing to remain in for too long. Julius has made that mistake before. There's something incredibly addictive about the way a woman lusts. He disentangles himself from Dave.

'Let's freshen up. I'll get you so hot… I want to see you as wet as I am right now.' It's all the convincing Dave needs to be towed into the ensuite. Julius is frenzied. Dave is easy to coax out of his clothes. In the steam of the narrow, motel bathroom, Julius manipulates Dave into the shower-bath— warm water; a cosy moist embrace for Dave's oafish, inelegant limbs. Julius giggles at Dave's ungainliness and watches as he palms his penis to erection.

Julius smirks. 'I've a surprise for ya.'

He turns. Bare feet slap on the tiled floor. Despite the steam, a chill in the air prickles Julius's exposed skin. The open zipper of his jeans scratches against the thin arch of his hip. His swollen nipples are pinched and tender with the cold that only arouses them further. The seam of Julius's jeans rides high and hard against his clitoris. The heat he feels is not from the spell he's weaved nor Dave's eyes on his arse as he squats to rummage through their discarded clothes. Coarse fabric rubs against his drenched vulva. His body throbs. It's hot hot *hot!*

Atomiser in hand, Julius stands, flashing a smile at Dave over his bare shoulder.

'Julie? Are you coming in?'

'It's not that sorta surprise.'

Julius approaches the tub with deliberate sensuality. He slips a hand into the front of his jeans, fingers gliding through the slippery folds of his vulva. His clitoris pulses appreciatively. Julius pretends it doesn't affect him. Nonetheless, he can't suppress a moan and Dave grins.

'You ready?' Julius pants, rubbing his clitoris with one hand, fumbling behind his back for the atomiser with the other.

'Uh-huh.' Dave blinks slow. He doesn't even see the bottle Julius brings to his face.

The fine mist of tink-spiked potassium is violently efficient. It ignites as if it's flint-struck. There should be sound. But there is only the hiss of the shower and Julius's delighted peals of laughter. Dave never knows what happens. The indescribable pain he feels as the flames devour his epidermis and dermis is as brief as his struggles.

Julius shuts off the shower, careful to avoid the water himself. Dave's screams are rendered all but silent, the tink lowering his voice into a bass-vibration too low for humans to hear. He feels Dave's agonised wails through his chest and legs as if they're coming from a boombox.

Limbs shaking, Julius feels his body melt back into its original skin. He slumps against the ensuite door and shuts his eyes. Dave's liquefying flesh sears behind his closed lids. He'd like to relax. But arousal has persisted into his male body, his cock thick and hard against his scarred hip. Fortunately, the high of burning someone alive still has him buzzing, and his temporary vagina's discharge still glistens on his erection. Self-lubrication is a glorious thing. Grasping his slick shaft, he strokes himself to an easy release. Drained, satisfied—he wipes his hands with Dave's discarded shirt and stands, his joints cracking. He tosses the shirt into the inferno of Dave. He gathers his belongings and exits the bathroom—the smell of burning human always reminds him of bacon. Panning for tink is hungry work.

Back in the bedroom Julius dials his client.

'J! How's it going? Got the good stuff for me?' Peter crows, with insincere camaraderie. Julius knows it's insincere. Peter has threatened him with a none-too-pleasant end more than once when Julius had failed to sniff out urgently enough his next *humine*.

'Only if you've got the money, Peter,' Julius replies. 'This is fine quality tink. I'm telling you.' Julius licks his lips. 'Tasted like vanilla and peaches. I'd know. Bastard had his tongue down my throat not ten minutes ago.'

They laugh. Peter asks about prices. Julius groans and takes the mint from on top of the motel's pillows. It cracks between his teeth.

He ends his call after arranging the sale. Humming, Julius imagines the burger he's going to make himself when he gets home.

When he no longer hears Dave's boombox vibrations in the ensuite he meanders over to inspect his handiwork. The tink ensured no smoke damage, but the ensuite's ceiling is blistered, paint peeling. The grout is cracked between the wall tiles. And there, amid the charred residue of the tub, is a modest pile of ashes. Tink.

12

Milk and Bread

Suzanne Hermanoczki

ONE:

'A story written in my mother's white ink' – otherwise known as – 'A matter of what had to be done'

'… she is undoubtedly a mother, but a virgin mother;
the role was assigned to her by mythologies long ago…'
– *Luce Irigaray*

Ever since I was a little girl, my *Abuelita* used to tell me this story about her mother, about my great *gran mamá, mi bisabuela*, Madonna.

'One day, the two of them were walking down the street on their way to great Tía Crispina's place. Tía Crispina lived in a well to do *barrio* on the other side of the city of Buenos Aires. It was a long walk at a brisk pace, but it was quicker still if they took a short cut through *Villa Miseria*.

As they turned down (the now renamed) *Calle Milagros*, they saw a poor woman sitting by the side of the dirt road, crying inconsolably. As they got closer, they saw clutched to the woman's breast, a tiny baby. It was such a poor shrivelled miserable thing. It was crying too, but with sound only for he had no more strength for tears.

My great *gran mamá* Madonna went up to the poor woman and asked her, '*¿Qué te pasa, mi hija?* Why are you crying so?'

'It's my baby,' the woman answered. 'My *niño*, my son, *tiene hambre*, but I have no more milk left to feed him.'

With tears streaking down her sunken cheeks, the woman held up a withered breast for both of them to see.

Under normal circumstances, *mi bisabuela* Madonna would have given her a couple of *pesos* from her purse and walked on by, but on this day, she took the baby from the poor woman's hands, unbuttoned her blouse, pulled out her own breast and, right there in the middle of the street, started feeding the woman's infant with her own milk.

Most would have been startled to the heavens at this point, but wait, there's more.

The instant *mi bisabuela* Madonna's breast touched the baby's lips, he stopped crying. By now, a small crowd of women from the *barrio* had gathered, first to see this *espectáculo*, and second to witness this unusual, older but respectable *Señora* baring her rather full bosom in public.

All the women of the *barrio* watched the infant suck and drink Madonna's milk until his cheeks began to fill out into ripe, pink lady apples. Then, his tiny body began to grow and stretch before their very eyes, growing so large he became too heavy for my great grandmother, so much so that she could barely hold him in her arms.

Only when the baby, now a small child, had fed enough, did he fall into a sweet sleep, the first time in his poor wretched existence, that mi *bisabuela* Madonna handed him back to his mother without saying a word.

'*¡Que Dios te bendiga!*' the poor woman whispered. 'Bless you!'

Buttoning up her blouse, *mi bisabuela* Madonna merely nodded and bid all the other women in the *barrio* a curt but polite, *'Adiós.'*

Resuming their path to Tia Crispina's house, *mi bisabuela* Madonna turned to my grandmother and said, 'I hope that one day, you will teach all your granddaughters to do the same.'

TWO:

El Sándwich Miraculoso

'... often interpreted, and feared, a sort of insatiable hunger,
a voracity that will swallow you whole...'
– *Luce Irigaray*

The first-and-only time, *la Virgen Maria* appeared to Don Mario was on a toasted cheese and tomato *sándwich*. It was her face alright, with that shroud thing over her head and everything. It was a strange sight to be sure, Don Mario, opening the sandwich maker expecting lunch but instead, seeing her holiness emblazoned on his bread! It was such a shock, he lost his *apetito*. He couldn't bring himself to eat it after that. Knowing he was about to bite chunks out of her divine head, he wrapped *el sándwich tostado* up in cling wrap and hid it in the freezer and thought that was that. But no way *José*. Every time he opened the freezer's *compartimiento para el hielo* searching for something, there she'd be, peeking out at him behind a packet of frozen vegetables. Some days, overcome by hunger, he'd clean forget, open the door and out would pop the holy toastie, landing in his hands, face side up, giving him a shock. That said, there was something funny about that too, each time he caught it, it was always warm to the touch, kinda like – *una tostada*.

At first, Don Mario tried to ignore her - her surprising him like that - until it happened far too many times to be *pura coincidencia*. So, he quit buying ice-cream and avoided the freezer section in the *supermercado* altogether. Then, he forgot all about her. Funny that, him forgetting *la Santa Madre* in his fridge. But see, that only goes to show you what kind of *hombre* he is.

Until the other day, when he was reminded of her all over again.

Don Mario was sitting in his brown La-Z-boy recliner, right in front of the old TV set when he heard this:

... And now wrapping up today's news, we'll finish off with a modern-day miracle. In today's 'This Crazy World' segment, Mr Luis Rodriguez, 54, a store owner in New Mexico has placed a crab-stick on permanent display after claiming it bore none-other than the face of Jesus. HRTV reports ...

'... Well... I'd just finished frying up a batch of crab sticks when I noticed something fishy on the last one. It wasn't cooking properly. When I scooped it out, it was there I saw a face, deep-fried into the old seafood stick!'

Then, they showed a close-up of the crab stick and sure enough, it was him! The bearded *Jesús!* The man who had experienced this *milagro* was waving his hands up to the heavens shouting, '*¡Aleluya! ¡Dios mío!* It's a miracle!' and other stuff like that.

... *The stick has even been declared a holy relic by the local preacher, Padre Antonio Domingo of Saint Augustino's church* ...

'Since that day at the deep fryer, hordes of people have been coming into my store with all sorts of prayers and *ofrendas*. Everyone wants to touch the crab stick. At first, I was afraid you know, that it would get damaged, or worse, someone would eat it by mistake, so I had this special glass viewing case built, to protect him.'

'The shop owner had the thing put on permanent display inside his take-away shop and is now charging five bucks a pop to come in and worship it! Sheesh!' thought Don Mario. *Really! ¡Por Dios!*

'I'm thinking of getting it insured, but it's been hard you know, explaining it over the phone. How much can a miracle like this *really* be worth?'

As Don Mario watched the TV segment, all sorts of people drifted into the man's little store, each one with a request or a *problema* that only Crabstick *Jesús* could solve.

'Please can you take care of my mother in heaven, she died last Saturday...'

'Please cure Tío Arturo's bowel cancer. I know it hurts him real bad...'

All these people praying to a crabstick, begging for their own little *milagro*.

As the camera was rolling, an ancient-looking lady came into the shop, dropped to her knees and started crying.

'It's him alright!' she shouted, crossing herself over and over, tears springing from her eyes. 'It's a *signo!* It's *el Señor!*'

'Not one person so far has said it wasn't him,' the shopman continued. 'And I can't help believe it too. That there crabstick is a miracle.'

... *Reports of the crabsticks' far-reaching miraculousness have also come in the form of scientific evidence. Professor Turino of the Department of Holy Relics from the University of Bologna was so taken by it that he came all the way from Italy to study it and his findings are nothing short of astounding* ...

'You see, the crabstick is perfectly preserved. Given the weather down there in New Mexico way, and the fact that the apparition happened about two months ago, the stick doesn't smell, not one bit. In fact, it's perfectly preserved. Our team of specialists have been monitoring it daily.'

… And in a place where even your own dear old grandmother will start to smell after two days of sitting out on the porch, this apparition has proven to be a 'real' miracle, not just for Mr Rodriguez but in fact, for the whole town …

'Yep, it's been pretty good all-round, especially for business, I got to say. We even have a bus service coming out to our pueblo every day. Now that's a real miracle.'

… Needless to say, most worshippers can't resist stocking up on Mr Rodriguez's fried treats, with many going away with at least three bags full …

'I even put a new item on the menu. It's called "The Holy Stick"—it's a deep-fried crabstick with a splash of chilli sauce for his beard.'

… To everyone in the town, Mr Rodriguez's famous crab stick has been a godsend …

'Last year, I was pretty close to broke. My wife had left me and I hit on hard times. I confess, I was not a good man. I was a womaniser and a drunk. I believe this was my sign from God, to turn my life around. To turn over a new leaf, like they say.'

… And now with all the money coming in, Mr Rodriguez is using his profits for good …

'With the money raised, Padre Domingo can finally make repairs on the school and I can finally afford to pay for my *Abuelita's* cataract operation.'

… But even more miraculous than that, is there hasn't been one complaint, health or otherwise, so far. And now back to the studio …

On hearing that, Don Mario jumped up out of his La-Z-boy recliner and went running to the refrigerator. After a year and a day of hiding, afraid of her Holy Toastieness, he searched the whole freezer—but she was gone! His 'good-for-nada-lay-about-I'm-never-leaving-home-ever-again-third-*testículo*-of-a-son' had eaten it only a couple of *minutos* before.

'Of all the things in there, you ate *that old thing?*' Don Mario asked him in Spanish.

'But Pa, I told you I was hungry. If our mother were still alive, she'd a fixed me up something hot and good. She fed me so well… Jeez, I miss her.'

'Ah son, you didn't notice anything um… funny about *el sándwich?*'

'Funny? Like what funny Pa? Funny ha-ha, you mean funny like that?'

'No… I mean… Did you see like… um… a woman…? I mean, was there a face on it?'

'A face? What are you talking about, Pa? All I saw was a sandwich that looked like a frozen hot pocket. Well, it did have some black things on it, but I scraped 'em all off. Was that mould? Jeez Pa, how long was that thing in there for? Before or after Ma died? I'm gonna get sick, aren't I? Answer me, Pa. I *am* feeling kinda funny now come to think of it... If only my mother were here, she'd know what to do... If I was sick, she'd cook me up some chicken soup with *fideos* or, I know, some *arroz con leche* with a sprinkle of cinnamon on top or a big bowl of...'

As Don Mario stood there in the kitchen of his tiny run-down housing commission house in Inala, staring at his 55-year-old son's greasy lips moving up and down talking about his mother, Don Mario's late *querida*, all he could think of was his miracle-in-waiting, his sign, the answer to his prayers, his golden ticket, his *el dorado*, his *gordo* – all swallowed up into *that* hole.

13

White Spaces

Reanna Kissell

I didn't know they made wood this smooth. It almost looks like a painting. The flowers sit atop the coffin as though they had existed for that very reason. She insisted they be brightly coloured, with only a few white. Didn't she know that in some cultures white is the colour of mourning? Isn't that what we are meant to be doing? The colours feel like they are mocking us for crying, only the white offers solace. It's best if I just focus on the wood. This shade of brown is one of my favourite colours, it matches the shoes I am wearing. Two miniature coffins attached to my feet. She is gripping my right hand now, holding it so tightly I can see it going white in places, as though my hand is what she is using to mourn. The priest is talking, do I call him that? I don't know his name, he is reading some sort of script. It's a round of mad libs but no one is allowed to laugh.

* * *

I can remember the first time it started happening. I was standing at a bus stop. A one-legged pigeon stared up at me with unsophisticated kindness and resolute calm. It wobbled slightly, readjusted its stump under its breast and stood tall on its good leg. The dusting white-grey feathers were matted against the poorer of its sides and yet there it was, unaffected. I don't remember kicking it. I don't remember the feeling of the impact, or the anguished cry it bellowed as it glided across the platform. All I recall is looking into its eyes and finding a sort of peace, followed by a missing piece of time. Was it a second, or a minute? I'm not sure. There was no one around in the moments after. Had I kicked it more than once?

* * *

When I remember him I feel more as though I am forgetting him. When I focus my mind on the memory of him the entire world is cigarette smoke, cheap beer and a sinking feeling that lurks at the edges of everything. Then I forget where I am. I don't know how long I slip away for to visit him. Sometimes I try to fight remembering, it's not always clear why I fight it, he is gone and the memories have already happened, they can't re-happen. Can they?

* * *

I think he is standing near to me, I can sense someone watching me. I am on a train, it is peak hour and I can feel the heat coming from the left of me. Is it him? I want to turn and confirm it for myself, I almost feel an imperative to do so, but my body is stunned into stillness. I am rigid, my skin cold. I feel like I can't breathe, something is sucking the air out of the carriage but no one else notices.

* * *

It is raining. The steps downward to the platform at Parliament Station are already covered in water. The traffic signal ticks over to green. Sheets of rain slapped down leaving the sidewalks slick with water. I was moving at a slight jog now, the water had reached my skin through my clothes, my hair was stuck to my cheeks, water droplets covering my glasses. I inhaled deeply and leaped over a puddle that had established itself as part of the road. Out of the corner of my eye, white shoes. For no more than a second. Then, an umbrella and the assaulting rain momentarily abated. The white shoes and then an umbrella, sheltering my last few metre dash to the steps. I didn't think to look up at the owner of the shoes. I was wet, I was cold, my train was due in a few minutes. It was only when I sat down in the carriage that I remembered the distinct smell of tobacco and the scent of mowed lawn.

* * *

Christmas Eve morning. It is somewhat cold for an Australian December, the day has the promise of warmth, the kind that will make your clothing stick to your skin and the chaffing in between your legs inflamed. I am lying in bed, I have only just woken up.

Something has woken me up. What was it? A sound? A smell? I glance to my right and Robert is asleep beside me, the cat curled up on his chest. They look so peaceful. The sun is shining through the shutters onto his side of the bed, my own side untouched. It feels early, untouched. It is the hour of morning that should not be disturbed. Why am I awake? I feel as though I have been beckoned into consciousness for something, someone. But all around me I can see, feel, smell only calmness, serenity. Then, the phone to the left of me buzzes.

* * *

I am looking at a photograph of you. If I squint my eyes I think I can see something on your shirt. It looks almost dirty. There is a greyness to it that I can't quite comprehend. Are they holes? As I stare at the photograph it is blurring, it's as though the edges of you and the background are merging, melting. The colours are changing. First, white. Then, a red hue emerging from behind you, like an aura around your body. It's getting stronger, shades of yellow and orange are blending together. It's getting darker, it looks as though you are burning. The marks on your shirt aren't holes, they are coals turning to ash. This cannot be real. You cannot be burning. You cannot be gone.

14

From the New World

Dai-An Le

HIGHEST-PLACING
MONASH UNIVERSITY STUDENT IN THE
MONASH UNDERGRADUATE PRIZE
FOR CREATIVE WRITING

Here is a pretty girl with pretty hair and pretty eyes, all black, black, black and glowing like a harvest moon. With skin as pale as the linoleum floors, she stands as a beacon in this room of yellow light. Lin watches her beneath the sweat of her brow, this porcelain doll of her dreams. Like a money packet draped in silken red, *qípáo* cut short, she seems, all at once, oddly perfect and out of place amongst the stench of chilli oil and stinging peppercorns. How breathtaking—Lin shrivels in her presence, unworthy of it all. Lin takes her shaking hands—from the cold, from her sixth cup of coffee today and fifty-second hour awake—and shoves them into the pockets of her jacket, bitten nails picking at its insides.

'Good evening,' this child born of the moon says. Her smile is practiced and perfect, teeth like pearls individually set into her mouth. 'How may I help you?'

Lin flickers her gaze down to the scuffed floor. Her toes peek out of her sandals, dark stumpy beetles born from her mother's flesh. She tucks them in like a turtle in its shell.

'Er, I'm here to pick up take-away. Under Lin.'

For a moment, time seems to stutter. The stretch of the young girl's fine mouth is a permanent fixture on her face. Lin thinks she sees a pinprick of light whir in the centre of her black eyes, an endless vacuum she could drown in. Lin shivers, feeling the chilling air a little more, hearing the ticking of the clock a little louder, beating in time to the beckoning paw of a *maneki-neko*.

'Yes,' the girl finally says and it comes out like a dial tone. 'My apologies. There will be a ten-minute wait.'

Lin nods with a slight twist of her lips in a mockery of an imitation and tries her best to be friendly but her body feels not her own and she tucks herself away into a corner instead. The room is a cramped little space, achingly empty and silent in the middle of a late, Wednesday evening. The floors have been polished, the vinegar and soy sauce untouched on each table and Lin wonders how long it's been since she has seen anyone here. Last week, she thinks, she saw a group of young girls in pleated skirts and white sundresses that the owner had fawned over. Uncle's broad fingers had looked like the roots of an elder tree as they splayed across their backs. Then, the week before, was there not a schoolgirl, red ribbon in black hair with brown island patches all along her arm? Or was that last month? Yesterday? The throbbing in her head starts up again and Lin thinks of her seventh cup of coffee and the unfinished project waiting for her at home—her little robot puppy, three-legged and hairless.

Outside, the gentle humming of the latest StreetCleaner consumes the silence. Long, spidery limbs burst forth from a silhouette almost human and it prods every corner, every drain and every pipe, piercing plastic bottles and scrap pieces of white cotton with its talons. Even the trashcan is something to be admired, the way it eats up plastic bags and cigarette butts to leave nothing, saying thank you in the end as if it's been done a favour.

Above, the moon gleams through a curtain of fine clouds. The wind, too, whistles mournfully, weeping trees dancing to its lullaby, their branches waving farewell. Lin shivers, watching the glow of red lanterns floating above it all like vengeful spirits. Even then, through the patches of frost on the window corners, the shop reflection shimmers in clarity. Plastic-wrapped food in miniature shrines, tatted, peeling paper dangling from the ceiling and that girl, that pretty china doll with black hair and paper skin—

She watches her.

Watching, waiting, to the incessant clicking of the clock and the murmuring of the wind outside. Then, her little mouth moves and Lin sees it in slow motion, hears it like a gunshot: help me.

The screeching of cheap table legs roars as Lin kicks in her seat, flinching back as if electrocuted. Screeching, and it rings inside her head too, rattling her insides until her stomach churns. She jams her eyes shut and sees floating lights dance beneath her lids, presses the palms of her hand hard against her ears until only her stuttering heartbeat remains. The wind stops. Lin sucks in a breath. When she looks back up, she sees only herself in the window. Little rivers run rapid in the whites of her eyes and dark spots gather all around a darker, sunken face. Just beside the entrance, the girl stands perfectly still as she had at the beginning. Her dainty hands are tucked in front of her and she stares at the door, waiting patiently.

'Did you,' Lin begins, and her throat suddenly feels too dry to be saying so much. 'Did you say something?'

Vacant, black eyes turn slowly to face her, as if noticing her for the first time. 'I did not,' she replies and turns back to face the door.

Lin nods more to herself than anything. Too much coffee, she thinks, even though those words still echo inside her head in haunting clarity, the picture of that mouth flickering in individual frames like a broken film reel. She peels a napkin from the pile and rips it up into pieces, catching that perfect, pale face in the corner of her sight. There is something so strange about her, this daughter of the moon. She stands so still and speaks in staccatos, disjointedly and slowly, as if every word is selected with the utmost care. Lin counts thirty seconds exactly and the girl blinks. Thirty seconds again, and she blinks. Again and again as precise as before. Lin can't look away. In her sleep, she must have seen this girl. She must have for her to be so achingly familiar. Not her nose, slightly upturned and perfectly small, as if chosen just for her. Not her chin, slim and delicate like a quail's egg. None of this by itself. Yet together, Lin feels something cold brew inside her, the simmering of a memory from another life. Perhaps an old friend from school or another student from college. Perhaps a reminder of an actress from a show she'd been recently watching. Perhaps.

'Lin!' A familiar face pokes out between the curtains behind the counter and Lin relaxes in her seat. The cheap, fake leather sticks to the small of her back where her jumper has risen. Uncle hands her a plastic bag, all ten spring rolls and sticky rice dumplings. His grin splits his weathered face like a cut in worn leather. With narrow eyes in a wide face, he is a sweet old man with greying hair all lined up on his sides. 'So sorry for the wait.'

'No problem, Uncle.' Then, in a quieter, hushed voice, because she can't help it, because she needs to know, 'New worker?'

Uncle's gaze flickers over to the girl, lingering a little too long. 'Oh, Mai? Yes, got her a couple weeks ago. Had to pull some strings but I think she's worth it,' he says proudly, eyes gleaming underneath the fluorescent light, and it hits Lin then, like a bullet train.

'She's an android,' she breathes. Her shoulders sag with a weight she hadn't known and she laughs all to herself, deep and guttural, a burst of uncontrollable peals bubbling from her throat. No wonder.

'Yes, you didn't know? Aren't you supposed to be studying them?' he asks, turning back to stare at his Mai, his little darling autumn bird. At the sight of her dainty figure, his mouth grows, lips stretch tight around yellowed, corn kernel teeth too big for his mouth. Lin watches Uncle's cheeks burn crimson. He always craved a daughter, didn't he? Always gravitating to the young girls bounding down the street, offering them food, telling them how pretty and refreshing they are, how much his son would love to meet them. A deep warmth spreads from Lin's calloused fingers to the middle of her chest and she is glad for Uncle. As a government official twelve years and running, his son visits rarely. 'I knew, from the moment I saw her, I had to have her.'

Lin stares at this doll from her childhood in awe, the prickling at the base of her spine long gone. Machines, she knows, and she huddles close until her nose almost grazes the silk of the dress. She lifts up an arm and the warmth from working machinery seeps through her, comforting in its familiarity. Mai doesn't move an inch.

'That's—that's incredible. I couldn't even tell. I mean, I had a feeling but—but god, she's so real,' she coos, admiring the little hairs on her face. 'I've never seen one as real as her before. The others—you can always tell, you know? The eyes are always so glassy and the skin never fits quite right.' But this skin—this skin is perfect, translucent enough for blue veins to show through, and it even rises from the chill of her fingers.

Uncle chuckles. He goes up to run the back of his knuckles against Mai's cheeks and rests his hand on the curve of her hip. Mai doesn't move an inch.

'Of course, she's the latest model. Mind you, these are still in the testing phase. Only got her because of my son.'

Lin hums as if she's listening, as if she cares for anything more than the machines that have raised her. 'Did you get her made after a celebrity or something?' she asks, fixed on the underside of that arm. A pattern of moles and splotches lie against the skin there, dyed umber. It must be common somehow on androids, some sort of subtle logo for a brand, for her to recognise, faintly, the way those brown specks spiral into a point. 'It's just— she seems somehow familiar. I don't know, like I've seen her before.'

'I'd hope not. These ones, they make them all unique. One of a kind,' he says. But Lin is sure. She is sure she's seen this face before, or some modification of it, hidden in the deep recesses of her mind for things of more use like codes and formulas and metalwork.

'Really? I swear—I swear I feel like I've seen her somewhere before, a while ago.'

Red lanterns, floral skirts. Dark hair pulled up high against filtered sunlight through orange trees. Scent of burning, scent of oolong.

'I don't think so.'

Pretty girls, lovely girls, all dressed up like little birds beneath an autumn sun. Flowing like water, smelling like cloves.

'But I—'

'Lin, have you been staying up again?' Uncle's voice reverberates.

When she looks at Mai, she sees only the pinnacle of robotics, a remarkable culmination of human achievement.

'I—' she begins but words feel too big for her mouth, the way they barely squeeze out of her throat. 'Only—only for a couple days. My project—I have to build a new type of robot from scratch, you see and—and they want it by the end of the year.' Uncle nods as if he understands anything about this world of robotics she has fought hard to find a place in. He pushes on the curve of Lin's back and leads her towards the counter. The rough pads of his hands dip slightly beneath the hem of her worn jeans and their heat is almost burning. Lin shudders, pulling back, but Uncle only presses deeper into her flesh, dragging circles along her skin. She glances to the door. Uncle's hand slowly falls away but the warmth on her hip and the indents of his hands linger still.

'You've got to take care of yourself,' he says. 'You know how you get when you're like this. So prone to imagination. Those movies, they get into your head.'

Uncle says imagination and it sounds nice, somehow, and safe. She latches onto it. 'I know, I'm sorry. Just busy,' Lin replies.

'Even so, there's always time to take care of yourself. Make yourself look nice,' he says. He pats her on the cheek with hands too hot and damp, dirt caked brown beneath the nails. Lin shudders at the way those lips peel back unnaturally, all dark teeth and empty spaces, and her feet shuffle back on their own.

'Just a moment,' Uncle hisses, thick fingers coming up to grip her jaw tightly. 'One moment.' Lin squeezes her eyes shut, watching spots dance beneath her lids, feeling a thumb run against her bottom lip. 'You know, you'd look quite nice if we fixed you up a bit. If you'd take care of yourself, I'm sure you could be a lot more useful than what? A student that makes fake dogs? How old are you again?'

Lin feels the table's edge dig against her thighs. 'Nineteen.'

'A little old,' Uncle says, and it lingers between them, acrid breath like unripe fruit. 'But still good.' Still good, he says, and Lin watches the glow of the exit sign burn behind him, its green clutch beckoning. Even then, Mai's skin shines brighter than it all and Lin grasps onto her like a lifeline, this pearl of Uncle's life.

'Do you know,' Lin begins too loud and too sudden, but Uncle startles as if awoken and that is enough. 'Do you know how they made her? Mai, I mean.'

Uncle hums, turning back to look at Mai who, even now, still stands obediently by the door. His weighted touch falls from her face and Lin breathes a little easier. 'What?' he asks.

'Do you know how they made her?' Lin repeats, a little more firmly. When Uncle steps back, she skitters away to where green light flares strongest. Mai's eyes flicker towards her. Uncle's lumbering footsteps chase her closely.

'Not completely,' Uncle says. 'If you're interested, you can meet my son. He'll show you, I'm sure.'

'It's just her skin and her face look so real,' Lin begins. 'She has little lines by her eyes too.'

'They make them very lifelike now, you know.'

'Oh, they even put a birthmark on her arm.'

'Yes. A minor flaw but I don't find it distasteful enough to remove.'

Lin shakes her head. 'No, not a flaw at all. It's a nice detail. I think those freckles are very charming. They look like—they look like scattered sand or—or—' but they sound too familiar on her, tongue, as if she's said those same words in a dream, to the same person, in the same place only—only—

'Your food is getting cold, Lin,' Uncle says and, lacking its familiar rise and fall, it comes out in a broken rhythm, pulled out through the holes of his mouth. Lin swallows, looking at a clock only just ticked over half past midnight.

'Right, yes. I should get going,' she says. 'I'm sorry, I've probably wasted your time.'

Tracing the freckles on the underneath of Mai's wrist one last time, Lin tries to imprint the softness of it all in her mind, the skin texture and warmth. She follows a map of green and blue veins with her fingers and presses in hard to see if they have given Mai its ridges too. A resistance like muscle, how wonderful, how detailed, and then, and then—a thump, thump, thumping. The clock stops ticking but she feels it still, a steady throbbing beneath it all. Slowly, Lin's gaze rises up into the cold, dark void above her and she sees herself in those eyes like a mirror, crouched low and ghoulish. When Mai blinks, Lin counts twenty-seven seconds before she blinks again. Then twenty-four, then nineteen, eighteen, fourteen. Her mouth opens, pink tongue poking through a row of straight teeth. No sound comes out but Lin has seen that exact mouth move in that exact same motion only moments ago. The arm falls from her grasp as she rises up with her entire body pulsating uncontrollably and wraps her hands around herself as if that, somehow, can ease the chill. When Lin takes a step back, a shadow is already nipping at her heels. Uncle's plump fingers like fat worms slide up Lin's shoulder and rest there. They squeeze just below her neck once, twice. She smells the stench of fermented beans and its hot, wet heat on her cheek.

'Mai, go charge up. Don't think we'll be getting any more customers tonight,' Uncle says, and though his voice is hardly as loud as a whisper, Lin feels it travel through her, a spirit awakened.

With a practiced ease, Mai nods, making her way into the corner with a grace and fluidity beyond gears and bolts and fine machinery. Slowly, she tugs a wire from the corner and pulls down the collar behind her neck. Lin sucks in a breath. A port. A small, round port lies at the base of her neck like every other android, as it should be. Mai plugs the cable in, settling herself down onto the floor and a faint, familiar humming begins as her eyes flicker green. Lin staggers back, her heart vibrating inside her chest, desperate to escape up her throat.

'You alright, Lin?' Uncle asks. He looks at her with all the concern in the world and Lin feels her stomach churn acid and bitter fruit from the thought that she had ever believed him to be anything more than a lonely, old man.

'Sorry. I thought—I just thought...' Lin buries her face into the sweat of her palms, smelling the grease from her unfinished work, the grime from countless nights awake. 'I think I need some sleep.'

Uncle, with his warm, crackled hands, rubs circles into her hip. He pushes the containers of food, forgotten and lukewarm, into her arms of jelly.

'I think so too. Go on home and get yourself cleaned up,' he says. He grasps her gently by the shoulder and easily anchors her trembles to a stop. 'Come by next week, alright? My son's coming to visit and I think he'll like you.'

With a heart still racing, Lin nods, heavy feet moving on their own as if dragged by a string. Outside, the StreetCleaner has stopped. Closed shops line the street like empty mouths and hollowed faces. Lin turns around one last time to see Uncle in his restaurant. Beside Mai's paper skin and slender limbs, he seems so much larger than she had ever imagined him before. She watches him run his hands against the silk of Mai's *qípáo*, the hem risen up against the milky expanse of her thighs from where she kneels. The large expanse of his hand envelops Mai's shoulder before running down to the dip of her waist. Up and down, up and down, and lingering on her hip. When he glances up to see Lin staring, his mouth pulls up to split open a face worn and wrung dry. He turns off the lights. The tepid glow of dimming streetlights and a cold moon remain hanging up ahead, unsatisfied and hungry. Through the window, a green light glows and blinks.

15

The River

Eleanor Maher

Two boys run down a dirt track, dragging sticks that trace lines behind them. They wear swimmers, triangles of fluoro green, their skin soft, chests brave, heading for the river. The resemblance isn't strong, but the way they use their faces—urgent, determined, silly—marks them as brothers, one big, one little.

As they run a distance opens between them. The smaller boy lags behind, working hard in gumboots a size too big. His feet smack about inside them like a dull cow bell. Ahead, the older boy launches into a puddle, shooting the shallow surface into the air. The smaller stops and squeals as he watches the water arc in the air, his arms thrown down and knees bent in delight. He sloshes in to join his brother and the boys hold hands, sticks forgotten, jumping up and down in the mud.

Their mother's voice catches up to them, weakened down the length of the path. She is yelling *Boys*, you've got mud all *over* you. They remain holding hands, looking back at her, the smiles on their faces uncertain as they seek her tone. Lucky we're on our way to the river, she says, and they scoop up their sticks, splash out, keep running down the track.

Gathering speed, the bigger boy looks back over his shoulder, checking that he is faster than his brother. He always is, the inches between them at this age stunting any competition. The little one has stopped to examine something on the ground, digging with his stick. The big boy gallops back to see what he has discovered.

It is a Christmas beetle, round and crisp, on its side, not moving. The little boy digs a circle around it, carving out an insect sized podium. Is it alive? Can he pick it up? He tests it cautiously with his stick. Brown, the beetle glistens rainbow in the sunlight. He pushes the stick beneath the earth and it moves the bug like a subterranean animal. The beetle rolls over and remains inanimate. Softly he closes his hand around it.

A buzzing suddenly in his hand and he screams and hurls the beetle to the ground. It lands at his brother's feet, who stomps on it, a reflex sparked by the screaming. Sandy dirt mixes with the beetle, a dull shimmering of guts and moisture. The boys look at each other, alarmed.

The little one scrambles to his feet and kicks his brother hard in the shins. His brother pushes him back with a yell and he falls over. A rock takes a chunk out of his palm. The blood forms slowly, coming from deep. Their mother is yelling *Boys* and this time they are in trouble. I *saw* you kick him Jack. What did you do that for? You've hurt your brother, he's bleeding. Apologize *now*.

Beyond the casuarinas, after the bend, the river courses inexorably. Jack presses his lips together and glares at his mother's knees. Blood trickles from both boys in places that will later be scars.

16

Highgate Continental Books, Records and Gifts

Mara Papavassiliou

She is talking to the boy endlessly. The boy and the girl are having an easy conversation as they walk through the park and up the street to a store called Highgate Continental. Their conversation is frictionless but also dry, probably because both their mouths are parched from nerves. The boy and the girl talk about 'X,' and then 'Y,' and then 'Z.' Topic 'Z' segues seamlessly into the girl's diatribe about the impenetrability of 'certain spaces.' Highgate Continental was a space that exuded such an air of impenetrability, being a place (the girl thought) for night-time dwellers to go during their day-time down-time. She wanted to know if the boy thought they should go in there, into Highgate Continental. The girl always felt nervous about going in there, would rarely go in on her own, would be kind of dying inside when she did, but maybe, she started, just as the boy offered courtesy assuagement of her concerns, it was just that she had a subconscious fear of tripping over the little step on the shop threshold, like doing so would be a repeat of high school humiliation, and that she was simply not cool enough to really gain admittance to or really be *accepted* at Highgate Continental. There are always some spaces, the girl said, which seem to haze you like that. It's something in the air, something that can come down to the specific aperture of light that emanates from the windows, or what can be suggested by a shop's opening hours. Like, if a shop is open from twelve instead of nine, that's a hidden suggestion that one should be asleep in those earlier hours on account of one's night-time proclivities, the participation in which becomes a prerequisite for general admission. The boy wanted to go in there, didn't he? Into Highgate Continental? The girl said she wouldn't mind going in, if the boy wanted to.

But the question came too late since by that stage there was no choice left in the matter. The girl had already touched the boy's hand in a light grasp to urge him into Highgate Continental, an excited, expectant prick which she hoped they would remember for the rest of their lives, long after the specifics of their dry, extended conversation up the street and park had fully melted into their brains' grey matter. That touch, which at the very least extinguished all decision-making faculties in the boy, rendering him entirely amenable to the girl's will to visit Highgate Continental, would stand out like the bright and jagged and precious cache of metallic things in the ambling magpie nest of their memory. The girl was sure of it, and sure enough the surety of her belief settled into an epic narrative of star-aligned romance, experienced as a swelling lightness in her belly, even while her mouth was going full-throttle, in a delirious high frequency prattle, on and on about how 'no smoking, no loitering' signs are actually veiled attempts to criminalise poverty, all the while she was emptily picking up, vacantly examining, and putting down the curated and varied merchandise of Highgate Continental.

17

Pigeon

Emily Riches

Davey is still afraid of birds. Even feather boas in artificial pinks and reds make his nostrils wrinkle. He's been known to roar at pigeons in the street, their sour stench rearing to choke him.

It began at the park. It was damp June, too cold to take off their boots. The sky was a blinding white. Davey bumped along towards the duck pond like a wayward kite, while Shae, small and determined, struggled to keep up. The ends of her hair were slick from sucking on them. Bags of frozen bread swung from their hands. The bread had a stale smell, as familiar as the place under the bathroom door where the carpet grew black mushrooms, or the shitty-milky scent of baby that still clung to the empty cot.

Their Ma's broad back led them. She wore a long skirt that went straight down on either side; it hid her blunt white shins but made her appear almost cylindrical, solid and imposing as a water tower. She smelled of old milk too. Davey sometimes thought of her as a nurse, with her enormous impersonal cardigan and blurred face, but knew this was because of all the recent business with the hospital.

As they reached the water, there was a strong odour of fish. Bird shit webbed the concrete edges of the pond, the flat grey water stretching to a green island. Birds advanced in a feathery flock, stirring up the surface as the children flung scraps of bread into their midst. Swans dove, hissing, while ducks and pigeons snatched scraps from each other's beaks. When the bread was gone their flat black eyes remained fixed on them, brooding and watchful.

Ma stayed at the water as Davey and Shae ran off to the pine forest. There they pricked each other with pine needles and watched as tiny spots of blood budded. 'Sprite bites,' Davey called them. Sprites were difficult to spot: they flitted and chirped, zinging from tree to tree. They looked just like grasshoppers except for their bulbous eyes, which were electric-blue instead of black.

'There! I saw one,' Davey whooped.

Shae sat still, eyes watering as she gazed at the trees. She turned a crumpled face towards him.

'*I* didn't.'

'It's there,' he insisted. 'You didn't look quick enough.'

Shae twirled a piece of hair round her finger and slipped the end into her mouth. 'Let's go to the oven,' she said.

The oven was really a pile of stones buried further back among the trees. It might once have been part of an ancient wall. A large stone had fallen and created a hollow inner space, which was always dry and smelt of cold stone and leaves. They thought of it as a portal to the fairy world. They left sacrificial drops of blood there and on rare occasions found things inside it, like a coin or a dried flower. Once, there was even a bird skull, delicate and mottled with skin.

Ma had a word for these marvellous gifts: she called them foundlings. Even bigger things, like babies, could be foundlings. 'Some women don't want their children,' she told them. 'Some women throw their babies away, like trash. But I find them and take care of them like they're my very own.' Davey knew this was somehow different from being a foster kid, as he and Shae were.

He knew Ma couldn't have got hold of the new baby anywhere except the oven because one day it wasn't there and the next it was: squalling ceaselessly in the cot, its inhuman face scrunched up like a demon's. The baby lived in Ma's room and it kept Davey awake all night with its catlike mewls and screams. In the dark, Ma thundered down the corridor to the kitchen for milk, returning every five minutes, but the baby never stopped crying. Davey lived life half-awake for weeks.

Ma forbade him to go to school when the baby came. He and Shae weren't allowed to leave the apartment: they lay on the floor all day scribbling or playing cards, like prisoners. Sometimes they'd play in the square of dead grass where the clothesline was, but it was a sad place surrounded by a tall brick wall, and they always ended up fighting. They didn't have a telephone.

Whenever anyone banged on the door, Ma told them to go to their room until the noise stopped. She burnt in the sink all official-looking letters.

Davey was glad when the baby was moved to hospital, even though he knew this meant something was wrong with it. He didn't see it go. It disappeared the way it arrived: unannounced. Yet now that it was gone, everything remained askew: even the foundations of the apartment had shifted to accommodate the baby and now couldn't be put right.

In the quiet, a strangled yell echoed through the pines. The kids continued playing until it rang out again.

'Was that Ma?' Davey asked.

They ran back to find their mother knee-deep in the greenish water, cradling something against her chest. She turned to look at them and her round glasses caught the light, flashing like empty mirrors. She had hiked up her skirt, and as she climbed out the hem dragged in the water. Davey was embarrassed.

'Ma,' he hissed. 'What're you doing?'

She ignored him and cooed to the thing wrapped in her big hands.

'Will we take it home, Ma?' Shae asked, skipping and craning her neck to see. Ma held the thing closer and pursed her lips.

At home, Ma lined a shoe box with newspaper and nestled the bird in it, so the children could finally get a better look. It was wizened, barely old enough to leave the nest. Its weepy eyes couldn't focus properly. Ma fussed over it and busied herself heating up the baby's old milk from the fridge. She dripped it into the bird's open beak with an eyedropper.

Later, Ma shut herself in her room, so Davey and Shae put themselves to bed. They were used to this: when the baby was there, Ma often forgot to bathe them or get them dinner. Shae used to sit outside her door howling, but gave it up when she got no response. They knew not to venture into her room; the light was never on and the floor was crowded with dark piles of bags and clothing, impassable as a forest or a labyrinth. Ma breathed at its heart.

That night Davey woke fitfully from a dream. There was an unfamiliar sound in the house, a subliminal thumping and fluttering. He crept from his bed and pressed his ear against Ma's door. From within, there came the sound of something beating, as though big moths were thrumming against a lightbulb. Beneath that, a low soothing humming, like a lullaby.

In the morning, Ma didn't emerge. Davey made toast for Shae and then left the house by himself without permission. He wouldn't go far, just to the park. You could see the tops of the trees from their apartment. At the pond, there were people on the far side, picnicking in bright-coloured parkas. Pigeons cannoned off at Davey's approach while ducks and swans carved wakes through the water and eyed him beadily. 'Feck off,' he shouted, and threw a few stones. He felt a bit better as the flock squawked and scattered.

He made his way to the oven and walked around it a few times, looking for fairies. Davey *did* believe in them, but he hammed it up for Shae. He knew all that widdershins stuff in books was stupid. Real magic was less obvious, harder to explain. The oven was real magic, for instance. Ugly and ancient, it sat crooked and cracked and half-buried in the earth, yet it radiated with a power he could only describe as 'old.'

He liked the forest too. The pines shot up around him, thicker than his body at the base and thin as pencils at their tips. The sky up there was a searing, dirty white. Sometimes he'd walk up and down the rows of trees, not thinking of anything, or he'd let one thought repeat itself over and over to the rhythm of his walking. But today he sat down near the oven and thought about this old magic. You could feel it in the air, the way you could feel the presence of the dead in cemeteries.

It was then that Davey heard the cry. A bleat really, small and quiet. It could have been animal but there was something in the voice that reminded Davey, unmistakably, of the baby. The sound echoed, and he crouched down to peer into the oven.

He saw something like a child, but somehow wrong: its fleshy face had broad swelling nostrils, and its skin was puckered and wrinkled like that of a newborn or an old man. Its bones seemed to bend the wrong way. A grey blanket swaddled it. That helpless cry came again, and, as Davey stared, it opened its watery eyes and looked straight at him.

As the thing held out a fat fumbling hand he recoiled, stumbling away towards the pond. He stopped for an instance but his legs forced him on. 'Sorry,' he whispered to the thing as an afterthought. As he ran, he realised what he'd thought was a blanket was a coat of dirty, straggling feathers.

Shae was snivelling outside Ma's door when he returned and shot him a reproachful glance as he entered. It quickly changed to surprise as he sprinted into the bathroom and began to scour his hands with soap.

For days Davey saw the creature's face in dirty dishwater, in his porridge, in clouds. Asleep, his sister's slack face distorted itself into monstrous features and kept him frozen and watchful, miles from sleep. He thought he could show Shae the creature the next time they went to the oven. But wouldn't it scare her? That hideous face... his skin prickled with disgust. Besides, a slippery inner part of him wanted to keep this discovery to himself. He knew in a way it was special; it had shown itself just to him.

A week or so later, when he got the guts, he snuck out again and approached the oven with trepidation. But the creature was gone. The hollow was bare and dry and reeking of feathers. Davey found himself disappointed, savagely so. He kicked at every bird he could see on the way home and couldn't bear the thought of the apartment with that closed door and the filthy pigeon behind it. If the baby ever comes home from hospital it'll have to make room in its cot, he thought spitefully. He stomped into the courtyard and stared at the wall, his eyes stinging with tears.

There was movement in the corner behind the clothesline. He wandered over, prepared to frighten another nesting bird and instead found the creature. Just as foul, ragged with grey feathers, it crawled forward on its elbows and knees. It turned its squashed face to his.

'Please,' it said, 'I crawl. I come. To you I come.'

Davey couldn't help it; he kicked out at the thing and felt his boot connect horribly with something brittle. He legged it upstairs and locked all the windows.

When he fell into sleep that night, he dreamt he was digging a grave for the baby. His mother watched him surrounded by a grey faceless crowd of mourners. He dug and dug, his hands sore and blistered, his back aching. His teeth chattered with cold but every time he stopped digging the crowd moved closer and he became afraid. Sometimes he lashed out at them with the shovel and they scattered like birds, but they always sauntered back, pressing closer than before. When the hole was deep enough, he leant back and said, 'Where's the baby?' Ma said nothing and he cried again, 'Where's the bird?' He didn't want his work to be for nothing. Then Ma pointed into the hole. There was already something in there, something small, feathered and muddy, huddled in a corner. He could barely look at it. It croaked his name.

A fly buzzed over his bed and he woke to the sour odour of rotting feathers. His clothes were rumpled and damp, his skin cold. Davey leapt up, feeling dirty, and pulled his jumper over his head. As he threw it down it ruffled the three feathers curled on his pillow. He stopped. His hands began to sweat. There were more feathers beneath the pillow. As he wrenched back his bedclothes he found the sheets smeared with muddy handprints and clumps of soil. Tucked at the bottom, unmoving, was a small grey lump.

Shae opened her eyes. 'You smell,' she said.

Davey's mouth was gluey with shock.

'What's that?' Shae had caught sight of the lump. Her eyes bulged as she crept over to inspect the broken body of Ma's bird. Its neck was twisted at an awkward angle and most of its feathers had been ripped out. Davey gulped and felt a quiver of fear convulsing somewhere deep in his gut. He noticed a trail of bloodied feathers leading from their room to the corridor.

'Davey?' Shae's voice was small.

Davey stared at Ma's door as though he could see straight through it.

'It followed me,' he said, his tongue sticking to the roof of his mouth. 'It got inside.'

'Davey?' she said. 'What did?'

He pointed at Ma's door and, as if summoned, Ma emerged from behind it. With a single word—'hospital'—she blew down the corridor and out through the front door. It slammed after her and they heard the deadlock click into place. The apartment fell silent.

Shae looked as if she would cry, but Davey saw his chance at once. He moved to Ma's door, his sister following.

'What are you doing?' she said.

'I'm going to look for the thing that killed Ma's bird.'

'What will you do?'

'I'll kill it.'

The forbidden door swung open. The darkness emitted a rank perfume of mould and domestic decay.

'Should we turn the light on?' whispered Shae.

Davey fumbled for the switch. The overhead light flickered, once, twice. With a loud crackle, it glared down upon a nightmarish scene. Garbage bags proliferated over the carpet like grotesque mushrooms, their bodies split open, clothes spilling from their mouths. The yellowed blinds were drawn and speckled with black damp. One wall housed an enormous fungus spreading downwards from the ceiling. A small lane had been worked between the bags from the door to the sagging bed. Another led to the farthest corner and the baby's cot.

Davey flicked the light off again, his stomach writhing, and the room returned to darkness. Shae refused to enter and Davey sent her as lookout at the front door. He swallowed and began to feel his way towards the cot, trying not to dislodge any gaping bags. What would he do with the creature when he found it? He thought about dropping it from the roof, hitting it with a spade or leaving it alone and abandoned at the oven, that magical stinking hole from which it came. He thought about running away.

When he began to gag at the stink of feathers he knew he was close.

'Davey,' the thing said. 'Davey.'

Without flinching, he dove down into the dark and grabbed the creature behind the wings. Digging his fingers into its soft sides, he hoisted it up and over the railing of the cot, then crashed back through the bags, out into the light. It thrashed in his hands, scattering feathers and hissing. It squirmed out of his grasp and managed to bite him viciously on the finger until he screamed and flung it away. They both crouched low, breathing heavily.

Davey was nursing his bleeding finger as Shae arrived. 'What's its name?' she asked.

'It doesn't have a name,' he spat. 'Now help me. We have to take it back to the oven.'

'But look.' She lifted its feathery arm. 'It's like Ma's bird. A foundling. We should look after it.'

'It *killed* Ma's bird,' he said. 'It's evil.'

'It's sick.'

He noticed a bruise blooming on the creature's cheek, the tread mark of his boot. The eye nearest the wound had crusted over with something yellowish and thick. The creature mewled plaintively.

Shae began hunting around for a cardboard box, finding one under the sink. She lined it with newspaper and tissues, then opened the fridge for a bottle of milk. Davey watched the creature's throat move as it greedily sucked the liquid down. 'I'm naming it Pigeon,' Shae decided. It leant its leering head on her arm.

Davey saw red. He tugged the box from Shae's hands, hauled open the door of the kitchen oven and shoved Pigeon inside. It scrabbled and screeched as Shae rushed at her brother. 'Stay away from it,' he screamed, and snatched a knife from the block. His sister burst into tears and barricaded herself in their room.

That night, Davey sat up on the lounge for as long as he could, guarding the oven and waiting for Ma to come home. There was no noise from the kitchen and he finally dozed, his sleep empty of dreams. When he woke there was a dim light under Ma's door, a mewling and cooing from inside. The oven hung open and Davey stumbled over to it. There was nothing inside but the stench of old feathers.

18

Flower Girl

Chloe Riley

She is doing the flowers when it happens. Roses, white as snow, a small vase of them on each table. Her dress is tight at the chest. She's already grown since it was fitted two months ago. Too old for a flower girl, but not old enough for a bridesmaid. It's a thorn that does it, tearing her skin, making a slit. She feels blood, warm and wet. It seeps between her fingers and runs down her palm. She has nothing to clean it but her own saliva. Her lips close around her thumb. She sucks, feeling like a child.

19

The Harvest Man

N'Gadie Roberts

'Why couldn't I have the chocolate donut for breakfast?' Caden pushed away his empty cereal bowl. He grabbed his Spiderman lunchbox from the kitchen countertop and placed it in his bag.

'Because your teeth will fall out,' said Marla.

The boy scratched his head, fingers meshing with his thick afro. 'What? But you eat chocolate all the time—*your* teeth haven't fallen out!'

Marla rolled her eyes and gave him a pointed look. 'That's because I'm a girl, remember? Our teeth are stronger.' She checked her iPhone for notifications before throwing it back into her tote bag. 'Plus I'm older. Let's go.'

It was Caden's turn to roll his eyes as they left the kitchen. 'You say that for everything… Just because you're older, doesn't mean you have magic teeth. That's not real.'

'Yeah it does—all girls do. When we mature, our bodies magically change and our teeth become immune to chocolate.' Marla winked as she stepped outside and locked the front door. It was a sizzling morning but a crisp wind ruffled the ends of her sundress. She seized Caden's hand as they took their usual route to Highgate Primary School. His mother used to walk him, but since she had died, Marla was the one to take care of him.

'What does immune mean?'

'It means… You need to read more books.'

Caden made a fist and struck Marla on her legs, unimpressed.

'Ow!' she chuckled as they ambled down Femi Boulevard. She scanned the street and smirked at the familiar display of young children in large schoolbags, like oversized turtle shells. An old couple lingered on their unkempt lawn, dressed in outrageously patterned pyjamas. They waved eagerly at Caden and Marla as they passed. Amidst all this, noise from lively traffic punctured the air meshing with the thick heat. Marla dabbed a handkerchief on her forehead and yawned, walking slower than usual. 'It's when your body can defend itself from something. So, if my teeth are immune to chocolate, it means they can't be damaged by it.'

Caden remained silent, thinking of the girls at his school. He was pretty sure that the only thing that happened when girls grew older was that they became more annoying and bossy—except Marla. She was really nice. She played UNO with him, showed him cool stuff on her MacBook and would let him lick the bowl whenever they made banana bread together. The memories tugged a smile from his lips as he counted the Jacaranda petals on the pavement.

The pair cut through the local playground and headed towards Tahrin Avenue where Caden's school was located. Unlike Femi Boulevard, Tahrin Avenue was an industrial area paved with uneven cobblestones and had suspicious alleyways branching on either side. Down one of these narrow streets was The Magic Shop. It was a gloomy brick structure with a juniper cloth shading its dark windows. Caden thought it looked like an ugly Lego building. There wasn't a spec of colour or movement about it and its neon sign was always fused. Dead.

I wonder if it ever gets lonely, thought the boy. 'Marla... Do you believe in The Harvest Man?'

'The one that lives in The Magic Shop?'

Caden nodded in response.

'Everyone does. That's why kids aren't allowed to go there. You know that, Caden.'

'No, but do *you* think he's real? All the big kids at school say he does ex—expemirents on people and removes their brain. But they've never seen him. Have you?'

'I think you mean ex—per—i—ments. I've never seen him either, but I know someone who has. They said that The Harvest Man puts the brain in a flower pot, until it grows into a head.'

'What! What do you mean?'

Marla stared ahead distractedly; she was less talkative today.

Caden frowned and tugged her hand. 'Marla!'

She blinked abruptly. 'Sorry—what was that?'

'I said what do you mean it grows into a head? And why does he take people's brains out?'

'Enough with the questions, young man. The Harvest Man will hear you if you talk about him. You should be thinking about school. Sing me your three times tables.'

Caden toyed with a button on his uniform shirt. 'Fine,' he muttered, looking back at the shop. One day he'd find out what lay behind its obscure windows. Everyone said not to go near The Magic Shop, even his teachers. A tingling sensation spread through his legs at the thought of coming face to face with The Harvest Man. *I wonder if he has horns... Or amazing powers like Spiderman. Is he a great big man dressed in big black boots like the kind Baba wears to work?*

'Is The Harvest Man a magician? Is that how he can take out brains and make them grow?'

'You've got a wild imagination. Three times tables—go!'

It wasn't long before Highgate Primary materialised into view. Caden could see his school's tall walls, daubed doors and the blue naughty bench that turned his bum into stone whenever he was forced to sit on it. Once they reached the school, Marla knelt down to give him a hug. 'I'll pick you up near the lollipop man, okay?'

'Okay.'

'And remember—'

'I know, I know. Don't bully anyone, and don't let anyone bully me.'

'Good!' Marla tucked a strand of hair behind her ear then stood up. She yawned again, looking faintly green. Normally it was Caden who was yawning and begging for a piggyback. 'Bye, Caden. Have a nice day.'

'Bye, Marla.'

Later that day, Caden was summoned to the principal's office, just after the lunch bell rang. As he trudged to the orange administration block, he couldn't help but think of all the times he'd thrown dirty tissues in the recycling bin, or used the teacher's only staircase. The word detention rolled in his head like a hamster's wheel.

'Thank you for arriving so promptly, Mr Kamara. Have a seat.' Miss Chartelot was a slim, bow-legged woman with droopy eyes that gave her a constantly hostile expression. Her office reeked of shaven pencils and new erasers. Shiny certificates, diplomas and quotes hung on the wall behind her desk. Caden sat down like a trained dog, breathing in the air of seriousness inside the room. His legs trembled.

'Don't worry, you're not in trouble. Your nanny called.' She paused, scrutinising him with sharp, beady eyes. 'She says you have to walk home today. She can't pick you up.'

Caden swallowed the tension piling up in this throat. 'Umm... Why, Miss C? Marla, umm, she always walks me home.'

'I am simply the messenger, Mr Kamara. You live close by don't you?'

'Yes... Umm but what happened to Marla?'

'As I said, simply the messenger. You can ask her when you get home. I want you to walk with the other kids, okay?'

Caden nodded.

'Good. You're dismissed.'

Caden returned to his game of Four Square with Abai and Lovejoy, pondering all the possible reasons why Marla couldn't collect him that afternoon. In the past two years she'd been his nanny, she had never missed a single day. *She said she was going to pick me up today... And she knows Baba doesn't like me walking by myself. Something must have happened to her. Maybe she just needs a rest because she keeps getting sick in the morning.* Caden thought back to how tired Marla had been when they were walking past The Magic Shop. His eyes widened, as he recalled their conversation. There was only one explanation: The Harvest Man had heard them talking about him. He'd taken Marla.

When the final school siren rang, Caden slipped off to his pigeonhole at the back of the class, while the teacher was instructing people to wash their paintbrushes and hang their art smocks. He took out a pair of scissors and shoved them into his pocket. If The Harvest Man had taken Marla, then maybe he was coming for him as well, which meant he needed something to protect himself with. The scissors would help him become immune.

After the lollipop man helped Caden cross the road, he took a detour to The Magic Shop. With Marla missing, this was his only chance to find out what really lay behind its doors. Several year sevens were walking in front of him along Tahrin Avenue, and he trailed behind them until he was alone on the street. Glancing over his shoulders, Caden veered onto the side street where the shop was located. Although the street was vacant, Caden could feel eyes pressing against his back. The echo of his school shoes slapping against the ground made him even more aware of how deserted this alleyway was. Caden's briefs started digging into the insides of his thighs and goose bumps kissed his forearms. Paranoid, his walk turned into a scurry.

Finally, almost fainting from the stench wafting out of three large skip bins, he reached The Magic Shop. Two dilapidated DVD stores flanked the shop, their greasy doors locked with giant, rusty chains. Who did The Magic Shop belong to? Was there a password to get in? How was he going to get Marla? Suddenly, Caden heard the rasp of a large bolt being drawn. He halted his steps and pushed his hand into his pocket, clenching the scissors until his fingers hurt. The door of The Magic Shop opened. Fear whispered against his neck, telling him to run. Unable to obey, he stood there. Motionless. A girl with thick hair staggered out of the shop. Caden knew immediately from her stiff movements that she was hurt. A man dressed in a tracksuit and black boots exited the shop.

The Harvest Man, Caden thought as he gulped. The Harvest Man held the girl's shoulders to steady her. They were both turned away from Caden, murmuring intently. Caden wanted to hide, but there was nowhere he could take refuge; this street had no trees, the huge bins were too far away. The girl began coughing and panting; it was an awful, lurching sound that made Caden's face twist in disgust. She wailed once and sniffed. Caden whimpered, and immediately the man turned around. Except for his eyes, a white cloth covered his face.

'What the hell you doing here, kid? Piss off,' his voice boomed.

The girl pivoted then gasped when she saw Caden.

'M-M-Marla?' Caden's knees trembled. The weight of his school bag threatened to topple him over.

'What? Caden! What on earth?' Marla drew away from the man. Her nutmeg eyes usually sparkled with excitement whenever she saw Caden, but this time they were puffy and red. She seemed terrified. 'Caden,' she heaved, moving towards him with clumsy steps. She had changed from her sundress and wore a long, swamp-green skirt. Caden grimaced; it looked rotten.

'What—what on earth are you doing here, Caden?'

Caden still hadn't moved. His leg muscles had lost all memory as he watched his nanny and The Harvest Man. Marla's face was like a ragged dishcloth that had been overused. She breathed in heavily, and it made him feel as though his teeth were being scraped across a China plate. Caden began to cry.

'Shhh. It's okay, Caden. It's fine.' The boy looked up as Marla edged closer to him. He didn't remember her being so tall and lanky, or her hair being so matted. Panic lined the inside of Caden's throat. His eyes darted between Marla and The Magic Shop. The door was open and The Harvest Man had vanished.

He must have gone inside. Was that really The Harvest Man? To Caden, he didn't look like a monster, just a scary, mean man. Marla on the other hand… She seemed different. *Our bodies magically change.* Caden thought of what she had said earlier. Was this what she meant? Did girls meet The Harvest Man in The Magic Shop to take their brains out? Suddenly a hand clamped Caden's shoulder.

'Caden.' Marla shook him. 'It's okay.'

'D-D-Did-The Harvest Man-g-get you?'

Marla slowly ushered Caden away from the shop, wincing with every step. Beneath her arm, the young boy's shoulders continued to shake. Tears pooled in his eyes, and his back was damp, like someone had splashed cold water on him.

'No, no. Why are you crying? I'm fine. And what are you doing here? You were supposed to walk straight home!'

Caden's cries grew louder.

'Aww, Caden. What's wrong?'

'The Harvest Man… He got you,' he uttered between trembling lips. 'And something stinks. *You* stink.'

'What? What makes you think that?'

'B-because I saw him—he—the man with the thing on his face. And—and you said that your body magically changes. D-does The Harvest Man take out your brain to make your teeth stronger?'

'This is why you were meant to walk straight home, dammit,' Mara mumbled. She played with Caden's hair and spoke in a sweet voice, as if she were singing him a bedtime song. 'Listen to me, Caden. I need you to do something for me okay? I need you to keep this a secret. You can't tell anybody about today—not even your friends or your dad when he comes home from work. Not even your teacher or your Spiderman toy. Okay? Can you do that for me, please?'

Caden licked the tears that had trailed down to his lower lips and nodded with a sniff.

'Good boy. See—I always knew you were a good boy.'

Neither of them spoke as they reached the end of the alley to join Tahrin Avenue. Caden peeked up at Marla's face, shocked and nervous. Her skin had a yellowish tint to it, and its usual rosiness had vanished. Sweat dotted her upper lip and her eyebrows furrowed with pain. She looked like a stranger.

'Did you die when they took out your brain?' the little boy wiggled away from her clasp, so they were no longer touching.

'No, Caden,' she chuckled. 'You don't have to be afraid of me. Listen, you were right. I did see The Harvest Man because I wanted him to help me. I had a part of me that wasn't working, and I needed to have it removed so I could get on with my life. I'm still very young. Getting rid of it was the best thing to do.'

'Why didn't you see a doctor? And why do you smell so bad?'

'So many questions. I couldn't see a doctor because this is a special kind of operation, one they don't do in hospitals here. It needs magic, that's why I had to go to The Harvest Man. And… Sometimes… Sometimes the magic stuff he uses to get that part out doesn't smell that nice.'

'Okay. I wanna go home. Walk faster.'

'Don't worry, we'll get there soon. I'm just really tired from today. Just remember what I said about the secret. If anyone knows I saw The Harvest Man, I'll be in trouble. I'll go away, and you'll never see me again. Do you want that to happen?'

Caden hesitated then shook his head.

'Good. And if you do tell anyone, The Harvest Man won't be happy, and he will come for you too.' Everything Marla told him made sense, but still he had a suspicion that she wasn't telling him the truth. Something else had happened in The Magic Shop. Something bad. He felt that tingling sensation creep into his toes as he remembered the white cloth around The Harvest Man's face. He itched to tell his friends at school the next day but didn't want Marla to be angry with him, or to go away.

As soon as they got home, Marla went straight to her room. Caden was forced to make his own snack and sit in front of the television alone.

'Marla! Do you want to come and watch *Grizzly Tales* with me?' he yelled an hour later. There was no reply. Caden rose from his chair and tiptoed towards Marla's bedroom at the end of the hallway. The door was ajar so he went inside. No one was in the room, but on her bed was a giant red stain. Blood. Feeling his vegemite sandwich rise to his throat, Caden rushed out of the room and ran into the bathroom. It didn't occur to him to knock. All he wanted was to get the taste of brains out of his mouth. He froze.

Marla was on the bathroom floor. She'd was crouched on the tiles like road kill, her cheeks a deflated balloon.

'Marla! Are—are you—you okay?'

The bathroom's venetian blinds were closed and under the harsh white lights, Marla's skin was the shade of urine. She clenched her teeth and moaned loudly. Tears welled in Caden's eyes. He felt as if he was staring into a corpse... It *was Marla*, he recognised her—her hooded eyes, high nose bridge that was slightly bulbous on the end, the dim scar on her top lip... But she'd lost something about her. Whatever it was, its absence was manifested in her sunken mouth and lethargy. The image of his mother's open casket struck Caden's mind. Marla was probably dying, just like his mother had. Struggling to grapple with this realisation, Caden clenched the doorknob. A crimson liquid spread on the tiles where Marla sat.

'It's nothing, Caden. The Harvest Man said my body would change a little, since that part of me is gone.'

'But... Why isn't the blood coming from your head? I want to tell daddy.' Caden crammed his lips together, squeezing his eyes shut. He'd never seen so much blood before, not even when he'd cut his hand in cooking class.

'Ahhhh, no! You can't!'

He pried his eyes open. Marla's eyes were saggy teabags. She was sweating intensely, as if she'd run a marathon. Her nose flared as she groaned. The bathroom didn't look like his house anymore, neither did the bathtub, where droplets of Marla's blood had gathered.

She cradled herself, crying. 'Promise you won't tell your dad, Caden? Promise me. If he finds out he'll make me—ah—' she gulped down a mouthful of air, 'make me go away. Do you want that to happen?' Marla met Caden's alarmed eyes.

'No. I—I don't want you to go,' whimpered the boy. The smell of copper wafted up his nostrils.

'You can't tell anyone,' Marla repeated. 'No one. They'll take me away.'

'I promise, I promise.'

'You know you can't break promises right? Or the Harvest Man will come for you as well.'

'I promise, I said!' screamed Caden, running out the door. He stayed in his room for the rest of the afternoon, unable to leave. When his father came home from work that night, Caden pretended to be asleep. He didn't want Baba to ask him what was wrong, in case he read the lies on his face like he always did. Although he had promised Marla not to say anything, he had to tell Spiderman.

'I know you won't tell anyone,' whispered Caden as he retrieved the action figure from his underwear drawer. Cupping his hands against the toy's ear, Caden told him everything that he had seen that afternoon. Spilling his secrets left him in a state of relief, like a tight muscle had been released. He climbed into bed and instantly fell asleep.

When Caden woke up the next morning, he found his father watching television. Something was wrong. Baba was never home in the morning. Mr Kamara looked up briefly then continued watching the news. 'Good news. You get the day off school today.'

'Why? Where's Marla?' Caden rubbed his eyes and then rubbed his grumbling belly. Staring out the window he noticed how empty the street was—everyone had already left for school.

After several minutes of silence, Caden realised his dad hadn't responded. 'Baba? What happened to Marla?'

'Well, ah, she's gone away.' Mr Kamara made a show of organising the papers on the coffee table before standing up.

'Where did she go? Is she okay?' Caden furrowed his brows, watching his father closely. It wasn't like him to withhold information. He appeared on edge... Tense. The way he sniffed every few seconds was a dead giveaway.

'Yeah, she's fine. Just had to go. Don't worry, we'll get you a new nanny soon.'

'Where did she go? Will she be back?'

'Enough with the questions, young man. Marla's gone and she won't be coming back. You'll understand when you're older.'

But Caden already understood. He'd told Spiderman, and now Marla was gone. A feeling of unease settled inside the little boy's chest. Terror crawled behind his neck, pinching his hairs. He remembered Marla's words. *If you tell anyone, The Harvest Man will come for you.*

The Man on Fire

Shamina Rozario

He lay there, supine, half sitting on the table,
Staring at me unblinking.

His face was brown and dry like a paper bag.
His eyes were round and white, blue and bold.

And as he lay there burning up in the fire,
I glimpsed an image in the sea;

Two monstrous eels sliding over each other,
Making love in the deep blue water.

The acrid smell of smoke in the air,
The man turned to ash and dust.

He did not utter a single word,
Nor a single cry escaped him.

And all the while,
In front of the isle,

The eels knotted amongst themselves,
As the man watched me when he died.

I Purchased Two Donkeys

Kishore Ryan

I mainly wanted the grown one but I felt bad
taking it from its baby so I took them both

I kept them in the yard and bought them donkey food
from the supermarket but no matter how much

I fed them they were always hungry they ate
everything in the yard and left it bare after

a while I noticed there was something different
about these donkeys they didn't have any ears

I took them back to the shop but the salesperson
informed me of the no refund policy

I pointed out that the donkeys were earless
and after some discussion it was agreed

that this was unacceptable and that two pairs
of donkey ears would be mailed to my address

within five business days I went home with the donkeys
and fed them and waited for the ears to arrive

22

I Went to Bunnings to Look for God

Gary Smith

Excuse me, I said to the young girl who has to stand there all day directing fools to tools, but I'm looking for god.

What god are you after? she replied, we have a few. Or you could try the church up the road.

I've already been there but that god wasn't the right size for my particular sins.

Oh, she said, well all the gods are in the top row of aisle seven, why don't you go browse?

I will, I said, thanks.

I checked out the vast array of gods—there were white gods with flowing beards, yellow ones with several arms, a fat smiling grey god. There were red gods, gods in animal forms and even a black ivory god for god's sake!

A very young man wearing a Bunnings outfit approached as I stood with my hand to my chin. Can I help? he asked, you look a little godsmacked. He gave a small laugh at this, thinking himself funny.

Can't find the god I'm after, I said.

What sort of sins do you commit? Very important, if you don't match the right god to your particular array of sins you'll be up with all sorts of guilt trips, self-loathing, weeks and weeks of penance, abstinence and god knows what. So, he said again, what are your sins?

Oh, the usual, I replied, a bit of fornication outside the guidelines, some gambling. Lately there've been a fair few lies to cover the other sins, you know how it is? I regularly pinch LifeSavers from the checkout at Safeway, a lot of coveting of neighbours' wives, yes, I'm into coveting on a fairly consistent basis. Oh, and there's this big secret sin from 1989.

What sin was that? he asked.

I'd rather not say, I replied, it's a secret.

Well, he said, you can't expect me to suggest a god if you won't tell me your sins.

I stole a blind lady's labrador, I said. My parents couldn't afford to buy me one so I pinched hers and tied my battery-operated Diggity Dog to her lead instead. It walked her straight out into Camberwell Junction… peak hour— you can guess the rest. So I really need to get that sin forgiven.

Well, the boy said, pretty much all of your sins can be forgiven using any of the all-purpose conventional Christian gods. They've become very cheap and come in a few varieties, though they're all reconditioned. There's nothing new in stock unless you want something rad like a Hillsong or Scientology god. Then there's the Catholic god, with a bonus son-of-god thrown in— we've got those on special this month… you don't have children do you? Good. And they're very good gods if you feel you'll be doing a lot of repeat-sinning. They have this special feature called the confessional—just walk in, say you're sorry, repeat some empty phrases five or six times and the slate is cleared. Then there's the Anglican and the Presbyterian gods, a Hindu and a Buddha—very reliable gods, good gods for grave sins, is how I'd put it. Or we have this ancient Egyptian god, or a Muslim god or a…

I put my hand over his mouth. I want the one true god, I said.

Well, he replied with a wink, all the manufacturers offer a money-back guarantee if their god *isn't* the one true god.

So I can take a god, try him out, and if he can't absolve my sins I can bring him back?

For a full refund! the boy said. Not only that, but we'll throw in a handful of ex-stock Mesopotamian fertility-gods to boot. How's that?

Wonderful, I replied, I'll take every god you've got.

23

The Visitor

Rebecca Starford

The lawyer had warned Jill that the house was run down. That her parents hadn't kept up with maintenance. To manage her expectations. Jill had not enjoyed these conversations over Skype. The lawyer, flat-faced and astonishingly young, spoke about her parents as if he'd known them; if he had, he'd have known her mother and father never worried about matters of appearance. Still, she was apprehensive as she stood at the bottom of the concrete driveway, her neck straining to take in the complete façade. The house may not have been palatial when she left, but it still had a long way to fall into disrepair.

The house was a Queenslander—an Ashgrover, to be precise—fronted with a gable roof to the right and sitting on a half-acre block. The fawn-coloured paint was chipped and worn in places, the pink frosted glass cracked at the bottom left-hand corner. The square-shaped deck at the front, still sagging in the middle, wasn't safe; Jill always thought it curious that her parents never had it fixed. It meant the three of them had never sat out there together to admire the best view from the house.

At Jill's side stood Andrew. He removed his hat and wiped at his brow. His face was still pink and his stocky legs were slick with sweat. Jill stared at the tufts of dark hair on his thighs—Andrew had never been good at growing hair. Not beards, or moustaches, or even the hair on his head. Her husband hadn't lost much in the years she'd known him, but he only managed to grow enough of it to cover his broad pate. He hoisted up his khaki shorts, tucking in his checked shirt. Why in summer did men always dress like small boys, Jill wondered.

'Are you all right, darling?' he asked, squinting.

Jill felt herself nod. 'Yes,' she murmured. 'It's just as I remember it.' It seemed an impossibly long way up the drive. They couldn't get inside, anyway: they didn't have the keys. Andrew wheeled his suitcase towards the letterbox in the shade where Rosie now stood, kicking at some loose stones.

Jill stared down the empty street. She had asked the taxi driver to drop them at the corner. Some instinct on that glary trip from the airport told her she didn't want him—or any stranger, for that matter—pulling up outside the house. It would be easier for him, she explained, indicating to the street sign, to get back on to the main road. All of Paddington was a maze of one-way streets, some as steep as ski runs. The driver obliged without saying another word, popping the boot, his gold chain jangling at his wrist.

'What time are we expecting this agent, then?' Andrew peered up the side path covered in orange and brown leaves. 'Only I think we ought to get something to drink. Something for Rosie? Is there a café close by?'

Rosalie Village was only a few hundred metres away, down another hill, but Jill said nothing. She didn't want him to leave. It was a curious feeling, almost like panic, as she took a deep breath. The air was ripe with frangipani starting to turn. She sensed the heat of the concrete beneath her sandshoes.

'Shall we just wait? She can't be much longer.'

As Jill said this, a silver Jeep cruised down the other side of the street, glimmering between the row of gums like a stalking leopard. The car stopped level with the driveway and the driver-side window came down.

'Jill?' A tanned arm rested on the door. It was Crystal, from Stilton & Rose. 'Won't be a tick. I'll just park.'

They all watched after the car until it disappeared behind the swathe of trees near the corner. The lawyer had recommended the real estate agency. They were a local outfit and had dealt with many deceased estates before, and after all the fuss with the coroner and the press it had been easier to be referred. But as Crystal approached the house, a clipboard under one arm and an elaborate glass water bottle under the other, Jill began to wonder. She couldn't have been more than twenty, with low-slung black trousers and scuffed ballet shoes, her hair bleached to the roots, straw-like, and tied back in a severe ponytail. What she supposed Brits pictured when they thought of an *Australian*.

Crystal gave them a friendly wave. 'Aw, sorry if I've kept you guys.' She pinched her eyes closed in earnest contrition. 'Right! Let's get you inside. Oh!' She hurried to the stairwell, blocking Rosie's determined assent. 'That front deck's a bit dodgy, did you know? It's probably safer to get you up one at a time. We don't want you falling through the boards on your first day here!' She laughed, revealing a gap in her small square teeth.

Jill went up first, admiring the seahorse tattoo on Crystal's ankle. The miner birds perched in the wattle along the fence line chirped maniacally. While Crystal examined the chunky set of keys, Jill trailed the corners of the deck, testing her weight on each plank. It felt sturdy.

'Mind that switchbox,' Crystal warned, nodding in the direction of the mains. 'There's some asbestos in there. Nothing serious. Just get it cleaned out in the next few weeks, yeah?'

When she found the front door key and held open the security door with her foot, Jill hesitated on the coir welcome mat, her knees locked. She had imagined this moment a hundred times on the plane from Britain. Her return to the house. No longer an occupant but a visitor. How fraught that relationship was, she had reflected sadly as she gazed unseeing through her window at the black night, and so it had seemed terribly important that she take back some of that ownership, some of the control, when she arrived back in Brisbane and encountered her childhood home once again.

But now that she was here she didn't want to go inside. Not with Crystal standing there beside her, or with Andrew and Rosie downstairs. Jill had no idea what this intrusion might feel like, what it might conjure her to say that she didn't want anyone else to hear. She gripped the aluminium handle.

'I'm sorry,' she mumbled. 'It's just so... *odd*. Being back here... after so long.'

'Oh?' said Crystal, incredulous. She pushed stray blonde hair from her eyes.

'Jill? Everything all right?'

Andrew's voice sounded hollow from the bottom of the stairs, and as Crystal stepped back Jill lurched through the front door. Immediately she found herself immersed in the smell of her parents. Sandalwood, and the faintest tinge of mould; it was unmistakeable, and Jill felt her chest constrict. Is that how I smelled? Does it ever leave you, that essence? Jill couldn't remember it. She took a few more cautious paces across the old polished hoop pine boards, the floor groaning. The house was largely empty, of course; most of the furniture had been sold off or dumped at the tip weeks ago, but there were still a few pieces she couldn't bear to part with. The piano. The Formica table in the living room. An old hand-crafted draughts board. The teak bookcase belonging to her mother and the Royal Daulton tea set. Some photographs. A painting hanging in the living room. Other items the antique shop hadn't wanted were stored under the house for future sale.

Jill drifted into the master bedroom. Her parents' bedroom. This room didn't smell of them but of the sharp tang of disinfectant: a few bottles of Pine O Cleen and a bucket hadn't been removed from the corner. Of all the rooms, thought Jill, this felt the strangest to be bare. It had never been a tidy room, for one thing. There hadn't been a time, in fact, when Jill had stood in the doorway and not laid eyes on ashtrays, scummy wine bottles, plates of half-eaten sandwiches starting to go bad. But it was warm, homely clutter, with those African masks hanging from the wall, piles of grubby kaftans in the corner and her father's desk covered in dog-eared books from the university library. Now the bedroom felt like a diorama missing half its decorations. But they weren't entirely gone, these remnants, Jill realised as she shuffled towards the middle of the room, her face tilted against the afternoon glare. Through the drifting motes of dust, she could make out a faint outline of where the masks hung, the indentation still discernible against the paint.

'You've been away a while, then?'

Crystal appeared at one of the small windows overlooking the neighbours' side path. She ran a fingertip over the grimy sill.

'More than twenty years.' Jill shrugged. 'In the UK. My husband... he's English. I've not been back till now.'

Crystal was nodding, her frown sympathetic. She held the clipboard tight to her flat chest.

'I've never lived away from Brisbane,' she said. 'I've thought about it. Moving to Sydney, or Melbourne... That's where people go, isn't it?'

Is it? Jill wanted to ask. How could anyone bear to live a whole lifetime in one city? Brisbane had always been a place of departure, never a destination—surely no one ever moved here from the southern states. Jill felt herself grimace and hoped the young girl didn't notice but, like the lawyer, Crystal's face was an open, untroubled one, half-smiling as she watched Jill move about the bedroom. She could hear Andrew and Rosie stomping through the back of the house, Rosie making some exclamation about one of the photographs ('Mum, your *hair*!'). Jill closed her eyes, for a moment overwhelmed by a pain in the back of her head.

Crystal remained at the window, her attention now drawn to the backyard next door where tropical-toned clothes hung from a line. Could she feel the absence in the house too? Her lacquered fingernails tapped against the clipboard. Jill wished she would leave, and at last she gave a long, salutary sigh and handed Jill the clipboard.

'If you can just sign these forms—' Crystal raised her voice as the Moreton Bay fig tree in the middle of the street began shrieking with the nesting bats—'then I'll leave you to settle in.'

Before they left England, Jill had arranged for the power and water to be restored to the house in advance of their arrival. But that afternoon, once Crystal had left and the white sun sank behind the cluster of creaking eucalypts at the end of the street, she discovered the showerhead in the bathroom was covered in mould, and this had cracked the hinge, sending an explosion of water in all directions each time the tap was switched on. It was too late in the day to call a plumber so they would have to use the claw-foot tub instead.

'Gross,' said Rosie, wrapped in a towel, staring at the large patch of rust where the enamel had worn around the plughole. 'It looks like one of those asylum baths.'

'Just sit up the other end,' Jill said, reaching over the ledge to turn on the bronze taps. The water ran rusty brown for a few moments before clearing.

Andrew had braved the last of the afternoon sun and trekked down to the small shopping strip for food and drinks. Though the old fridge was still plugged in, Jill couldn't bring herself to look inside and find the ingredients of her parents' last supper in the house. They weren't big eaters; her father had never seemed to subsist on more than red wine, radishes and digestive biscuits. After the bath filled and Rosie closed the door, Jill wandered to the tiled sunroom next to a small alcove at the back of the house. This was an annex—her parents had built it themselves after she was born, extending the house by about five metres from the kitchen. It had always been her favourite room, cool from the tiles and almost subterranean with the three windows positioned level with the backyard that ran on a steep slant.

But Jill could hardly see outside: the grass was over two feet high, and new tangles of shrubs and weeds clogged the back fence. The old hills hoist still loomed in the middle of the yard. Jill put her head against the glass and took a deep breath, overwhelmed by a surge of fresh grief. Her mother, who had so little pride in most things, had been proud of her garden, spending hours out there, digging away at her vegetable plots, pruning the geraniums. During school holidays she permitted Jill to pick the tomatoes, aubergines, sweet peas and carrots and sell them from a trellis table out the front of the house. There wasn't much trade along the quiet street, but some neighbours gravitated towards the stall and Jill usually made a few dollars, which she dutifully bicycled down to Milton to deposit into her Dollarmites account. Why had she given up on the garden? Jill wondered as she traced an outline against the glass. She could picture her mother out there, one foot braced against the slant, a hand on her hip, an enormous straw hat casting her face in shadow.

'We'll need to go barefoot all year,' Rosie huffed as she padded out from the bathroom, leaving wet footprints in her wake. She did a twirl in the middle of the living room, slapping her palms against her thighs. 'And there isn't even anywhere to *sit*!'

'What's that, darling?'

'It's so noisy. The *floor*.' Rosie was staring at her with contempt. 'Didn't it drive you insane?'

Jill couldn't remember. The house had never felt like something they had inhabited but rather another part of her and her parents. Rosie wouldn't understand. Back home they lived in Swinbrook, close to the Windrush, in a converted Georgian stone cottage. Jill and Andrew had bought it soon after they were married. The exterior of the house had been in good condition, with a Stonesfield slate roof, but the inside needed shelling. Andrew had run the renovations, fitting out new appliances, the oil-fired Aga, the French doors. Out the back of the house were three acres of untamed garden running to the edge of the next farm. Jill had tried to maintain it, but she had none of her mother's dedication. She supposed she would need to learn about plants and soils and water now, there was no getting away from it; she'd have to look it up on the internet or go to the library and borrow some books, and she could already feel impatience at this task prickling in her bones. Jill thought about her garden in England. It never needed maintaining; it seemed to grow with refined disorder. Jill had always hoped Rosie might like a horse, or a dog, to inhabit it—to make it, in turn, habitable for the family. She had imagined roaming the garden with Rosie after school with this dog, a loyal terrier of some variety, making a path down to the creek. But Rosie never ventured outside unless it was absolutely necessary; she preferred the rumpus room at the back of the house where Andrew had set her up with a television, an iPod dock and a karaoke set she dragged out whenever girlfriends came over to stay. Sometimes Jill would find herself studying her daughter as though she were a stranger. They didn't look much alike—Rosie, more like her father with her dark hair and heavy-set brow, never inherited Jill's spray of freckles, or the fine line of scars across her knees and shins from a childhood outdoors, exposed to all that grit and grime. No bitten-down nails, no dry skin at the elbow. Rosie bore the complexion of an easy life spent indoors: she was pale, unblemished as fresh milk.

Jill glanced at her daughter now, frowning. It wasn't her fault she had never known what it was like to share space with others. Her parents' house wasn't a big house like Swinbrook. The bedroom at the front was large, though it opened right on to the open-plan living and dining area. There was little privacy, but there was also little separating them from the house itself; the surfaces were unfinished, rough to the touch. When she was a girl she used to lie awake at night listening to the groan of wind through the floor and walls and roof. 'That's the house breathing,' her mother would say, which always sent a shiver of fright up and down Jill's legs.

There was another room next to the master bedroom that her mother had used as a studio, and next to it had been Jill's bedroom. She peered around the jamb. The built-in cupboard with the brass handle was still there, on the left of the door, but the low-set desk beneath the louvre windows had been removed, the grimy outline still marking the spot. She watched Rosie drag her suitcase inside.

'So, you've picked my old room?'

Rosie shrugged. 'I thought Dad was getting the beds delivered. Where are we going to sleep?'

'We'll go shopping tomorrow, sweetheart. The timing for delivery was tricky with our flight...'

Rosie wasn't listening. She had slumped on to the suitcase and began picking at her toe.

'There must be swags downstairs,' Jill said brightly.

'Downstairs?' Rosie's head snapped up. 'In that creepy cellar thing?'

'It's not creepy. It's just a bit dusty.'

'Yeah, and full of snakes and spiders and whatever else can kill you in Australia.'

Jill smiled. Every now and then she could hear her daughter's accent. *Oss Tralia*. Jill had never lost hers. It didn't bother her so much now, but when she was Rosie's age she wanted nothing more than to throw over her drawl and become English. During those lonely Brisbane summers, she used to shut herself away in her bedroom and talk to herself in an accent, reciting her favourite lines from *The Young Ones*: 'Neil, the bathroom's free. Unlike the country under the Thatcher junta...' It amused her parents, this play-acting; they never saw how Jill was clawing to get out of her own skin. That this was the first hint of her one day leaving them.

She had once tried to describe these feelings to Andrew, but she wasn't sure he understood. They lived fifty miles from where he grew up; he still visited his mother every Sunday, and his brother stayed at the house at Easter with his Polish wife, Eva. His family had a pleasant, uncomplicated affection for each another, and Andrew had an uncomplicated relationship with his past. Everyone Jill knew in the UK assumed a childhood in Australia to be an idyllic one—'What was the problem?' a writer friend once asked. 'Too much sun?'

Jill, feeling spoiled and ungrateful, but also confused, had tried to push Queensland out of her head. How could she make them understand that it was possible to feel crushed by too much empty space? But when Rosie had been small, perhaps in a fit of homesickness, or nostalgia (for surely homesickness implied she longed to return), Jill began telling stories about Brisbane and found she rather liked it. About catching frogs at the stormwater drain at Norman Buchan Park, swimming in the river at Corinda minutes before a bull shark nipped a boater's finger off, the diamond adder curled up in the manhole in her bedroom, sugar gliders warring on the roof. The endless stretch of ocean to the east of the city, and flat, barren scrubland to the west.

Rosie never tired of these stories, either, and for years kept a map of Australia pinned to her bedroom wall with coloured tacks marking the places she wished to visit. It was only later, when Rosie had grown out of the stories and stopped asking when they would visit the grandparents she had never met did Jill reflect more on what had made her leave.

'Why don't we take a holiday?' Andrew often suggested. 'Visit the reef. Do Sydney. Climb Uluru.'

'You're not supposed to climb it anymore.'

'Well, *look* at it, then.' He never pushed her, though. Andrew wasn't intrepid; Europe offered him more than he needed outside of drizzling Oxfordshire.

Jill went and stood at the flyscreen door. She wondered what had become of Andrew and felt a flutter of panic in the pit of her stomach. It happened from time to time, this worry for Andrew, and for Rosie. It was anxiety, she supposed, or some other kind of animal instinct, for now that her parents were gone Jill didn't have another living relative. She propped open the front casement window. The hinge was stiff, but the wood finally gave, and she pegged the snib into place. There was no respite from the heat. These timber houses had no insulation, and the air crept in through the gaps in the boards. In winter they would be cold—colder than in Britain; it was all relative—but Jill hadn't warned Andrew or Rosie about this. She could see the mosquitos fluttering at the top of the stairs. Low, tinny music from Rosie's phone sounded from Jill's old bedroom.

She turned, leaning against the ledge, and raised her eyes to the ceiling rose. How many times had she looked at it as she lay out on the untreated floorboards, the test match crackling on her father's radio, the ply-panelled Fisher air-conditioner on wheels gurgling away in the background, the steady drip from the mesh vent falling near her head? She stepped away from the window to examine the painting hanging on the wall. Her parents had never been connoisseurs of art, but Jill had always admired their eclectic taste. She didn't know this artist, though she liked the style. It was large desert landscape, pale blue and grey sky marbled with solid cloud. A small, washed-out mountain range receded in the distance, while thick oils in the foreground had rendered a clump of impenetrable spinifex, clay and blood clotting the base of the shrub.

What had drawn her parents out there? Jill still hadn't allowed herself to pick at that question. Why had they got into their old Pajero and driven over two and a half thousand kilometres to Alice Springs, and then to Tennant Creek where they parked by the Old Police Station waterhole? The detectives said they'd taken no food or water, no mobile phone, much use it would have been out there. It made no sense. Perhaps one of them had been sick, Jill pondered, reminded of a cat she once had, Pushy, the ragdoll her mother brought back one afternoon from the Ipswich pound. Pushy was already old when she arrived, with only a few good teeth, and when she decided it was her time a year or so later she had gone under the house to die. Jill had found her, eventually, when she began to smell. Is that what her parents had decided to do? Take themselves off in a ghastly unceremonious gesture? They had never liked attention, abhorring any kind of fuss; theirs had been a quiet existence, and Jill always considered this to be dignified, something to emulate. But this, she thought, taking a deep breath. *This* was monstrous, and despite the heat she shivered suddenly.

'What were they doing out there?' Andrew had asked when she got off the phone after the consulate had called. That had been eight weeks ago—it felt like longer, like years; grief had the habit of stretching out time like elastic. He had been crying, though Jill knew it wasn't for her parents, who he had only met a few times, but for her—the startled, ugly crying of a child.

'They like to travel,' Jill had said, flicking on the kettle. She felt unreasonably calm, almost weightless. 'To explore.'

'To the desert? Without food or water?'

Andrew had been staring at her, incredulous, and she realised he expected her to have answers to this mystery, that after all these years she could still discern the workings of her parents' minds, and in that moment she experienced a searing jolt of loathing towards him for burdening her with that responsibility, that expectation. With that guilt.

Jill turned her face to the last thread of sun between the trees. Somewhere down the street she heard the *thunk* of a cricket ball on a bat. The sound of afternoon traffic drifted down from the main road. A car drove slowly by the house.

She never thought she would return to the house. She had counted by the years in England proudly. Five, ten, fifteen… She had felt nothing on these anniversaries—no tug from home, no regret. She telephoned her parents a couple of times a year for birthdays and Christmas, but since they refused to learn to use Skype she had not seen their faces for such a long time. Her father occasionally sent postcards from obscure locations around Queensland, addressed to Rosie, never a word of greeting to Jill. *Pamela and I spending a pleasant EKKA holiday in Roma, met a charming red heeler at the pub; Are staying on Great Keppel at Svenden's resort on a far end of island, away from jet-skis and déclassés…* Jill sensed the reproach in this correspondence, the sliver of spite, but she always smiled as Rosie pinned them to her wall beside that giant map of Australia, all the time wishing her parents had written to her instead.

'You'll be back,' her mother had said all those years ago as Jill climbed into the taxi bound for the airport. Her father had stood on the deck, a mere shadow, refusing to come downstairs. She had never seen them so angry—their fury made the house glow in the pale moonlight. She was twenty-three years old and had just finished her doctorate. She had never been in love. She hadn't understood all the nuances of betrayal back then, or how easily, and wilfully, her parents could uproot her sense of belonging. Jill had not realised her mother's words might have been a warning.

24

In the Stuffing

Hannah van Didden

'Leave the machines running.' The man in the grey suit spoke over the flatline tone from the back of the room. 'I need the body when you're done.'

'Time of death: eleven eleven.' The doctor's eyes remained on the display even as he withdrew the stethoscope. 'I'm sorry for your loss,' he said. 'That must have been hard for you to see.'

'There was nothing more to do,' said the man, unfolding himself from wall to bedside.

'Now, Mr Leverman.' The doctor nodded, rolling the stethoscope into his coat. 'I must admit to being somewhat curious. What is it you're going to do with her?'

'Her body? I'm going to stuff it,' said Mr Leverman. 'You see, I'm a taxidermist.'

'I thought you were a banker.'

'Robotic taxidermy is a side venture of mine. Animal subjects to this point, but I'm branching out.'

'Ah, but that explains how you've stayed so cool.' A knowing look swept across the doctor's face. 'You haven't really lost her then.'

'I've signed the release for the body and life support systems.' Mr Leverman produced a set of papers from inside his jacket. 'You may appreciate I need to get started as soon as possible. I have a van waiting.'

'Certainly, Mr Leverman. And good luck to you.' The doctor motioned to his nurse. 'Make the necessary arrangements.'

'Thank you, doctor.' Mr Leverman dipped his head and, by the time he raised it again, the door handle had twisted to a close from the other side.

Alone, the widower could inspect his late wife in peace. He traced a finger down the side of her face. So serene.

In the lead-up to this day, there had been so much angst that he'd almost forgotten the inner sweetness that drew him to her in the first place, that empathic tilt of her head, the floating to her walk. She could have been an angel, if it wasn't for all that red hair.

It was the last weeks that killed them—her declining health and tolerance.

'I can't believe I left Roy for you,' she'd screamed, after picking up to the mystery caller.

He'd told her 'that woman' meant nothing, apologised for the powder— one measly bag of Argent M, for goodness sake!—and still this background-blending worm of a woman was making plans to leave. Him!

Without him by her side, she was a common daisy browning into the ground. She really was. Poor little Cherry.

The door flew open. His eyes met the nurse's and he pressed Cherry's hand to his mouth. Then he was striding to the goods lift, following the mechanical in-and-out of the mobile life support system and the trolley with its cranky wheels.

* * *

The body lay spotlit in the centre of the room, the aching gasp of the respirator accompanied by regular blips until the observers approached.

'You sure she's fresh dead?' One of the two peered at the body over rimless lenses. The raise of his eyebrows was a caterpillar stretching. He ran his fingers across a cheek, a forearm. 'Her dermis is exceptionally dry.'

'That's my Cherry. She was sick before she— Look, Mathias, I was there. I did everything as you said. Can we just get started?'

'I will begin shortly, Mr Leverman.'

Mr Leverman licked his lips, a constant habit on account of the Argent M that Cherry had so despised. 'Leverman is fine,' he said. 'And what's this "I" business?'

'Leverman—' Mathias revelled in this. '—you cannot be here for the curing. For this process, I need solitude.'

'If that's how it must be.' Leverman frowned. 'But you must talk me through it.'

'Very well.' Mathias circled the body with measured paces; his client followed close behind. 'First, I will inject liquid metal into her marrow.'

'Liquid metal? That's a bit non-descript.'

'Bone metalliciser. A proprietary secret. After that, I'll flush her blood and spinal fluid and replace them. And, before you ask—'

'Let me guess. That's proprietary too.'

'It's to stop her cells from degrading. The skin must be prepared according to a strict regimen—none of your old metho and borax, thank you very much!—to keep intact her circulation, nerves, organs.' The technician stopped mid-tread and turned to his client. 'What are you going to use her for anyway?'

'Everything she used to do,' Leverman said, leaning closer, 'and more.'

Mathias cringed at the warmth on his cheek. 'Well, then. I'm certain you'll be disappointed if we stuff her with the Homebot 32C you've got there. It has particular… limitations.'

'I was under the impression—' Leverman's speech was cut by Mathias's upheld hand.

'I'm not saying we can't do it, because we can. We can pull her skin over a metal frame, which is pretty much your 32C, and she'll look passably human. But she'll act like a robot. You would be able to tell and it'd get to you. It wouldn't be the same as stuffing, say, a finance guru.'

Leverman's face puckered at the technician's wink.

'Or,' he went on, 'I could use the latest seed model, the size of a chicken's egg. You're old enough to remember those, aren't you? Attached to the heart, I'd hardly have to rebuild. Plus it's a shorter process. Twelve hours, start to finish. And the tech's adaptive. She'd move, talk, act like she always did, but better. You've heard of the Stepford Wives?'

'I may have seen the remake of the remake.'

'She'd be perfection robotified. No one would be able to tell. Aside from a few tweaks.' Mathias jiggered the caterpillar above his eyes. 'So tell me, what did she do for a crust?'

'She was a teacher. Head of Human Biology at the University of Calligonium.'

'An academic. Lots of inhibitions then.' Mathias chuckled; his client remained stony-faced. 'This model I'm talking about is the most advanced of its kind, but it's under development.'

'What do you mean?'

'Pre-release. They're calling it the Kairos.'

'What a brilliant stroke of luck!' Leverman laughed and slapped the technician's back so hard the glasses jumped from his face.

'Did I miss something?' Mathias readjusted himself.

'I've bankrolled development of this little baby, but I had no idea it was ready. Looks like it's time for a little return on investment,' Leverman said, and the technician returned his smirk with an uneasy smile.

* * *

'It is done. All yours, Mr Leverman.' The bank manager leaned over his walnut desk to clasp the other man's hand with vigour. 'This is the part where I would ordinarily congratulate my client, but under the circumstances...'

'A relief, Bodkin, is what it is. Thank you.' Leverman rose and Bodkin followed suit.

'Your wife was a wealthy woman.' Cherry was born into money. 'What are you going to do with it?'

'I'd like to honour her memory,' Leverman said. 'We planned investments together.'

But that wasn't quite true. Maybe because of her pre-ordained fortune, his wife was loyal: she rarely said a negative word about him—except when it came to his projects.

'You're dangerous,' she would tell him.

'I'm a calculated risk-taker,' he'd respond. 'You, my dear, are the dangerous one. You forget I've seen you at jiu jitsu.'

She laughed at his joke and continued to give him a surface trust. He had listened to her ideas for one of his side ventures, after all, and this had led to their household's most functional appliance, a gadget he called the Need Machine.

The Need Machine was a palm scanner fitted to a black box. It read thought patterns and biomarkers to realise the object its user most required, by producing it in three dimensions. The Need Machine was useful for many things, from generating new batteries and car parts, to cosmetics and household chemicals. It took mere seconds of focus for the machine to interpret the user's problem and fabricate its perfect solution.

It infuriated him when Cherry used it, because it was never to its full potential. She only ever used it to conjure new cleaning products.

'But it gives me what I need,' she'd say, and he would grunt his disapproval.

Leverman envisioned much bolder possibilities: he saw in his invention the capability to create actual wealth. In its present form it was too crude a replicator, too limited by cheap feeder materials to form gems, precious metals, or cold currency. Yet.

On the day Cherry found the Argent M in the box, she was ropable.

'This box is wrong.' She spat the words at him. 'Get rid of it.'

'The machine or the drug?' he'd asked—and my how she glowered! Then she walked out.

He pocketed the Argent M and shifted the Need Machine into the garage, fitting it into the void behind the tool rack, a chamber he kept to himself.

Her reaction to his interest in robotic taxidermy for humans was met with similar displeasure.

'The subjects are dead, my dear,' he'd argued. 'It's like the law says: *no lights, no rights*. And it's not like I'm killing them for the project.'

'It's unethical,' she said, 'like the dodgy derivatives markets of the 2000s.'

'It's nothing like that. This is all above board. We've got legislative dispensation.'

'Speculative fiction, more like! Given the choice, I'd rather build a casino in the clouds.'

'That can also be arranged,' he said, and he led her to believe that was the end of it, this talk about his latest investment.

It wasn't, of course.

His pet project continued, swallowing every cent he had, but he could not speak further about it, particularly when the chief engineer had gone radio silent on him.

Her death was timely. He needed this money. She would never have bailed him out, not when she was posturing to leave.

Now her funds were his, and she was a robot. The thought brought him to smile, ever so briefly.

While roboticisation had made his wife more agreeable overall, the last days had come with new developments he didn't care for. Yesterday he had watched her leaf through a butchery manual to prepare stuffed spatchcock from scratch, after which she'd manoeuvred the knife around the bones with greater dexterity than he had managed in seven years of taxidermy. She was tempering his instructions—his dinner request had actually been filet mignon—and was beginning to show signs of unusual strength. He could still feel her fingers in that morning's grab of his forearm.

'What was that for?' He'd retracted his arm to rub it down.

'You were leaning across a searing hot pan,' she said. 'You could have burned yourself.'

'Thanks,' he murmured but, with his wrist cold and already purpling from her touch, he didn't feel thankful.

That act, coupled with last night's rough sex, had him spooked—but it was her suggestion of a more equitable housework arrangement that was too much to bear.

There was no question: Cherry was not herself.

Any drawbacks of the Homebot 32C looked decidedly attractive in the face of a potential throttling by his robot wife. He would take her back to Mathias to sort her out, that was what. But he'd tried calling all morning, to no avail.

When Leverman returned home from work that afternoon, his wife was missing. On the dining room floor was a card for Royston Canto, Robotics Engineer at the University of Calligonium.

* * *

Leverman slunk into the green-washed lab and slapped the engineer on the back of his campus-branded polo shirt.

'Roy, my main man. Good to see you.'

'Watch it! I'm mid fusion.' Roy steadied himself against the box that held his working hands. They were sheathed by thick gloves embedded in the glass of a tinted octagonal prism. Behind the glass was an unmoving creature the size of a large rat. Closer inspection revealed it to be a miniature spinosaurus.

'Soldering? I remember that.' Leverman pointed out a tool on the floor of the box.

'Undergraduate science was painfully impure.'

The probe inside the box touched to the dinosaur, which shook itself to life and ran at the glass. Leverman jumped back.

Roy slipped his hands from the gloves and looked up at his visitor. 'Dinosaur DNA and lab-grown flesh. Unpredictable when combined with conscious robotics.'

'Fascinating.'

'I think so. But that's not why you're here, is it?'

'No,' Leverman said. 'I'm here about my wife.'

'You won't find her here.' Roy cast his eyes back to the dinosaur, which was whipping its tail and gnawing at a limp glove-finger. 'I did see her today, in her old lab, but she's long gone,' he said, in reaction to Leverman's wandering eyes. 'I thought I was hallucinating at first. I heard she passed on.'

'She did. I had her stuffed.'

Roy smoothed his thumb and forefinger over the curve of his greying moustache. 'Which seed model?'

'The Kairos,' Leverman said, and the engineer simpered in response. 'What? Do you know something?'

'That's classified.'

'Even to the chief patron of the project?'

'You're TGL? You must be proud.'

'I guess. Maybe. Should I be? I haven't exactly been kept informed.' He glared at Roy, who ignored the look.

'But Cherry. She's magnificent, isn't she?' Roy puffed out his chest. 'We're at the bleeding edge. You have to admit, it's nifty tech.'

'I thought so. Until she started… changing.'

'As well she should. The technology's adaptive. ED. Evolutionary Design. It is Cherry, only better.' At Leverman's expression, he added, 'The robotic core is evolving as it fuses with Cherry's cells. Her brain.'

'Her brain?' Leverman's neck and face were blotching red.

Roy nodded. 'Every organ preserved.'

'So it's my wife's DNA, her mind, her memories, that this robot is based on?'

'It is her. Everything that once made Cherry, well, Cherry has been reactivated.'

'Without the inhibitions,' muttered Leverman.

'She's becoming a superhuman version of the person she was. No need to eat or drink. No sleep. Superior intellect, strength, speed. The capacity to excel in every pre-existing ability. There's no need for our cells to degenerate, did you know that? Especially not when they've been integrated with technology like this. And Cherry is one of the first to live it. This is an exciting step. You must be thrilled to bits.'

'Thrilled is not the word.' Leverman crossed his arms. 'It's a massive deviation from the process I agreed to.'

Roy crunched down his brow. 'You knew it was a test model, right? You signed the papers.'

'But I would never have agreed if—' Leverman wet his lips and encroached on the space of the other man. 'Who else knows?'

'Your technician. Some doctor from the hospital.'

'So much for confidentiality.'

'He came here asking questions. It did make me wonder...' Roy stepped back to the box with the dinosaur. 'The doctor's how I found out about her passing on. No one here was told.'

'It was recent. And sudden,' Leverman mumbled. 'But aren't you going to tell me what to do? Isn't there a way to stop her?'

Roy didn't seem to hear. In the glass box, his gloved hands lifted a probe, tapping the dinosaur's temple with a 150-milliamp charge. The creature stopped mid-movement and dropped motionless to its side.

* * *

'Hello?' he called.

Stiletto heels tip-tapped on the entryway tiles. She was home earlier than he'd anticipated. Fortunately, he was prepared.

'Sweetheart, it worried me when I saw you weren't here. Where have you been?'

From behind the kitchen door, his rubber glove-lined hands gripped a foot-long rod—a metal torch pincered to a battery—through which coursed a 150-milliamp charge. This contraption was what his Need Machine had produced, and he thought he had the gumption to use it. With her arrival, however, he faltered. He pressed tongue to lip, as though that would stay his rattling nerves.

'The shops were mayhem,' she said.

'Oh?' Paper bags rustled. A clever ruse. He reminded himself she'd been at the university without his say-so. This thought rekindled his ire. 'Come into the kitchen. I want to show you something.'

He thrust the torch at the space where her head should have appeared. The blow delivered, he geared up to follow through with the lethal shock: she emerged rattled but unscathed, a slimline helmet over her curls. He froze in place long enough for her to regain her bearings. She stretched her neck in a series of metallic clicks.

'You'll have to excuse me. I'm a little stiff today,' she said.

He raised the torch and she stopped his arm with her own, gripping until the torch dropped at her polka-dotted pumps.

'I thought this may be the case.' She tutted and removed her helmet to a flock of corkscrew curls. Then she slid a hand into the pocket of her apron.

'What do you mean, honey?' He spoke in a squeak, his field of view red with cherries, curls, rage. Her breath smelled of acetone.

'You still want to destroy me.' She whipped a syringe to her face, squirted fluid with the release of air from the needle. 'But I can resolve that, my husband, by taking care of you as you did me.'

'Sweetheart?' He held up his hands as a shield and felt a stab in his arm. 'Ouch!'

'That wasn't so bad now, was it?' She extracted the needle and deposited it in the incinerator chute.

He snatched back his arm and rubbed over the spot. 'What did you give me?'

She sweetly grinned and selected a knife from the block, the one he'd claimed for skinning and boning.

He rose to his feet, flattening himself against the kitchen cupboards, sidestepping his way past her.

'Run, my love, while you still can.' She scraped the knife on the steel as she coursed his trail with an unhurried sweep. 'In a moment, you will feel not a thing.'

He scuttled down the hallway in a stumble across tiles-then-carpet, snatching rear-view glances into the glass of picture frames on the way. He stopped for breath under the mounted horsehead in the living room and eyed off the stuffed animals around him. He pressed on a dog's paw, a cat's head, two bats, a wolf. Each stuffed animal activated and lurched in turn with snarls and bared teeth.

Cherry swatted away each of these with dignified ease, the result of which was a growing line of sparking fur behind her.

'I tested my own blood,' she said. 'They took samples before I passed on, but they didn't know what they were looking for.' Underfoot, she crushed a squirrel whose glowing eyes flickered to black at the floor. 'The syringe in the drip. You were clever, my dear. Making the doctors think I'd gone into respiratory distress.'

'For goodness sake, Cherry, I was just helping you along. You were dying.'

'But that was you too, preparing me little by little. All that bitter tea you made me. The regularity of the poison.' She laughed, raising wide arms to her shoulders. They were in the bedroom now. 'If I'd have known I was being set up for this, I might just have gone along with it. For I am eternal, my love, and you are mortal. An insignificant, little speck on the world.'

'Crazy bitch! What did you give me?' He collapsed on the bed; his legs, leaden weights; paralysis, rising.

'Why, it's your drug of choice—though at a substantially higher dose than your usual habit. It's what you gave to me, remember? And just look at me! Super, am I not?'

His arms stilled and she stood over him, the tip of the knife at his neck.

'You can't kill me.' He let out a snicker and talked himself breathless, sensing his tongue was about to disengage. 'You need me to legitimise yourself in this world. You can't spend your money when you're dead. And that's what you are—dead! Nothing more than a robot. You can't buy or sell or own a thing. You do not legally exist!'

'I may not, my love,' Cherry Leverman said amidst his dying laughter, and she opened the closet door to the hanging carcass of a Homebot 32C. 'But you do.'

* * *

Timothy Leverman marched to his briefcase, bent down, clenched a hand around the handle, bent up, turned to his wife, pressed lips to her waiting cheek.

'See you. To-night. Sweet-heart,' he said.

'You're syncopating.' She patted his face, her nails in the same shade as the marascas on her frilled apron. 'Is everything all right?'

'I'm. Fine.' He contorted his neck to face front, unblinking.

'We'll spend some time tonight working on your speech patterns and how best to salvage those investments of yours,' she said. 'I have such a mess to clean up. Be a sweetie and bring a lovely pay packet home. And try not to talk too much if you can help it.'

'Yes. Dear,' he said, drawing the door to a soft close behind him.

Cherry Leverman held hands to her hips and tilted her head. Even the sight of the blood clotted down her white cupboard doors couldn't darken her smile.

stuck

lou verga

there are two mes
me who experiences shit
and me who writes
about it. sometimes
they become one
an eclipse that numbs
fingertips

until experience me runs off,
sinking in thick substance,
thinking to survive alone. invariably
it crawls back,
sopping through bone,
and sobs on the familiar linen.
other me, shackled to the desk
slowly shakes its head
and says with its cold,
gaunt glare:
'you did it to yourself again.'

26

Mariang

Jeanne Viray

I usually dream in the third person.

I tried explaining this once, drunk, to the taxi driver. How it feels like my dream is a movie being played on a screen. That it's not mine but still *mine*. I'm a giant figure in the sky looking down at my doppelganger's teeth falling out.

'Weird,' he said.

'I know.'

I said teeth falling out meant that I was probably having trouble explaining something personal. He explained his own dreams were always in first person, and that his last dream had been his ears melting and, now, what did I make of that?

'Maybe you don't want to hear something you should hear,' I said.

'Hmrph. What was your last dream?'

'I saw a girl on a mountain.'

'How'd she look?'

I shrugged, forgetting he couldn't see me. He asked again. I said she was beautiful.

The driver asked me to tell more stories. I told him the story of how, when I was a baby, my family took me out to the new shopping mall, and I began to cry so much my *lola* believed *nausog ako*.[1] *Lola* believed bad energy had been given to me by a stranger, and the way to expel this was to pass me above a tub of boiling hot water, through the steam. I couldn't remember any of this but I imagine a scene of oriental magic: the withered hands

---

1   *lola*: pronounced 'loh-lah,' meaning 'grandmother.'

of old Asian women, a screaming baby passed through thick, grey steam, murmurs of prayers, fairies and old gods blessing the baby with happiness, the baby emerging on the other side, smiling and free.

He didn't believe any of it. At the end of the drive, I thanked him for getting me home safe and he thanked me for the stories.

Of the people in this particular story, I will begin with Daniel. Daniel, with the blue eyes. Daniel, who dated me first. Daniel, who dreamed of girls on mountains. Daniel, meeting his lions. Daniel, who dreamed of Maria.

* * *

She told him her name was Maria when they met at a ball.

Daniel attended things like that. Balls. Dinners. He used them for networking; as a student, this was very important. This particular ball had been hosted by the law students' society, funded by the university, attended by both students and staff. On the same night Daniel met Maria, I was at my own party in a rented hall celebrating my cousin's debut. Daniel and Maria ate three-course meals, with a choice of either lamb or chicken Kiev for dinner, and I ate from a banquet of food in silver trays, with *lumpia*, the meaty spring rolls on high demand, and *sinigang*, the smell of the sour soup making my mouth water, and *pancit*, of course, the pan-fried noodles in the middle of the table, a must for long life. Daniel and Maria listened to a paid, professional DJ. I listened to the church band.

I thought about how Maria was one of those who made it hard not to fall in love with her. I called it love because that was what she was made for, but others might just call it a 'pull.' Everyone had their own name for it. I was no expert in such things. I avoided love as much as I could—especially when I had it. Such aloofness made things difficult with Daniel. My fondness for him at the start didn't last and I understood when he left me because Daniel wasn't like me at all. I might've called him kinder than me if I didn't know what was in his mind while we dated. I hardly met his expectations of a Filipina.

That night, Daniel swirled his drink, shifted his feet, and took a deep breath to gather more cool air. He prepared and he steeled himself. He let himself be pulled by Maria. Fuelled by the lessons he'd learned with me, as soon as he met her, he wanted to keep her. Maria was always easier to keep than me.

She told him stories that made him laugh, and she was beautiful on his arm, with her long, dark hair and soft, *kayumanggi* skin.[2] But, most importantly, she listened to him in the way we all like to be listened to sometimes. He had her undivided attention.

When she grinned, she didn't blink.

'I once owned a mountain,' she said.

He laughed. 'A mountain?'

'I'm not joking.'

'Is your family rich or something? Can you even *own* a mountain?'

She made him dance with her, and then she took off her shoes and made him hold them. I'd seen Maria dance before, in a white *saya* dripping with mud and dirt.[3] She preferred to dance like leaves swirling in a wind-storm. In my bedroom that night, when she got home at two in the morning, she showed me how they danced, her hips bumping against the corner of my bed and my dresser, and she didn't listen when I told her to be quiet or else she'd wake up my parents.

With Daniel, she danced as he expected her to. He asked her again if her family was rich, and what was she doing here if she owned a mountain, and was she *rich*?

Her smiling mouth and thorn-like teeth barely moved when she spoke.

'Rich in my heart, maybe. Rich in kindness.' The way she said 'kindness' made him want to kiss her. She smiled so brightly, he didn't notice that her bare feet were crusted with fresh earth. Their dance left marks all over the floor. They danced until his feet bled.

* * *

When we first arrived here, I wanted a pet. Anything to make me feel like this life was different and better than the one I had before. Twelve years old, my mother took me to Queen Victoria Market on a sweltering hot day, hopping off a crowded Elizabeth St tram. Heat was dry here, not humid. The hot air rushed to our faces when we left the cool tram and I remember

---

2   *kayumanggi*: to have a brown complexion.
3   *saya*: also known as *baro't saya*, this is the national dress of the
     Philippines, usually worn at formal events.

a symphony of groans. But the market became my favourite place as a child, reminding me of crowds and smells that I'd forgotten, my nose led by fresh barbecue and roasted snacks, my ears led by the shouts of vendors. There was food, fresh fruit and veg, hobby stalls, bronze Australiana statues cranky old women told me not to touch, and a styrofoam box of ducklings.

Looking back, I'm sure it wasn't legal. My mother didn't want to keep them inside the house so we kept them in the backyard. In that unit, our first home, we had a backyard that was barely the size of our Ford Escort and most of the space was taken up by the washing line. The ducklings stayed in their box, my primary school uniform dripping over them as we left the ducklings' food and water and said goodnight. We forgot it was winter. In the morning, we found them dead, with a red fox picking at their carcasses. The fox had gotten through the fence.

My *Ate* Cora scolded me for wanting the ducklings in the first place.[4] Didn't I *know* the red foxes were out here? Shouldn't I have *known* that bringing the ducklings would bring the foxes? The fury in her eyes shocked me, her words booming at me: didn't you even *think* for a second, Nina?

She snapped at me too often back then. Everything I did was wrong, as if she had the rulebook on how to fit in properly in this new country. Now everyone would think we didn't take care of our animals, she said. Her directness stung and confused me, as if we didn't used to keep our dog in a cage by the street, before it ran away. I wondered what it was in the Australian air that made her so forgetful and stressed and unkind. I began to think this was the real *Ate*, hidden all along under the guise of a kind sister who would help me learn songs and share her dessert.

Maria told me not to blame *Ate* Cora. This was just her reaction, and she would settle soon enough. It was fight or flight or freeze. This is what happens when we're displaced. I don't remember what I chose for myself, but it made sense. Maria told me: remember, the foxes were brought here too.

* * *

---

4   *ate*: pronounced 'ah-teh,' this is a kinship term used to address an older sister, or older female peers.

On the plane, they taught us to fasten our own air-mask before fixing someone else's. What they didn't teach us is what to do when you're asleep and dreaming of homesickness one minute—and the next, the woman sitting next to you leaves for the bathroom and doesn't come back. Instead, a teenage girl does. But you're a teenage girl too, so it's okay. There is nothing dangerous about teenage girls.

Before Daniel met Maria, I did.

She sat in the woman's seat. I noticed dirty knees under her hemline. Her hair was unkempt, longer than mine. She held something tight in her hand, as tight as my mother held her rosary. When she breathed, I smelled Laguna air, which is thick like the scent of the ground after rainfall and the musk of an impenetrable green forest, yet riddled with smoke exhaust.

Cabin lights flashed on and off. The girl sat hunched over. I was sixteen.

'Where are we going?' she asked.

I told her where.

'Why?'

I told her why.

I didn't have time to wonder who she was or how she got here. All I knew was I didn't want someone sick next to me. She didn't know how to fasten her seatbelt when the time came, so I did it for her. She held my hand as we landed, and I held the vomit bag to her mouth when she vomited. I still remember the warmth of the bag, the slosh of the liquid inside. She had never seen so much metal before. It made her mad.

'Why am I here?'

I pointed at my sister, twenty-one years old then, holding hands with a pale man wearing khakis and a protruding belly from all the food he ate on their honeymoon. Cora Johnson, née Mercado, and Robert Johnson. I hoped that was enough of an explanation, I couldn't be bothered talking about it after weeks of preparing for their wedding and dealing with everyone. Maria closed her eyes again, the crease in her brow deepening and I finally offered the Vicks I had in my bag.

That must have been the fourth round trip we've made since moving to Melbourne. I was used to the turbulence and the smell of the airplane.

In the car, no one noticed the extra girl in the backseat. Whenever I tried to catch Maria in the reflection of the rear-view mirror, all I could see was myself. Maria's hair was itchy as it stretched along the backseat, touching the back of my neck, and my sister's, and her husband's. No one could find the source of the itch. *Ate* Cora and her husband bickered. Maria pursed her lips. She asked if I thought it was real love. I told her, nah, it's pretty bullshit. I remember now, I was the one who taught her the word 'bullshit.' She finally showed me what was in her hand. A ginger root. She told me to put it in my pocket. She whispered, 'thank you.'

By the time we got to the house, I had already made plans to keep the secret girl in my room. I would steal my dad's extra folding bed. I'd sneak her dinner. I hoped she'd like my clothes. I figured she liked dresses but I only had mini-skirts and I was going through my fishnets phase. I wanted to take her shopping. I wanted to show her the records I'd bought. I did all these things with her eventually, which Maria did enjoy, to her great surprise. But when I opened the car door, she was already gone. And in my pocket, which felt heavier and weighed my jeans down below my hips, was a gold nugget in the shape of the ginger.

* * *

Maria became my teacher when I was eighteen. She told me she knew a lot about love, and that it would be an ongoing lesson. She pointed out my mistakes with Daniel, and rectified them when it was her turn.

There was a way to love, she said. She taught me its history, and how it should be, how humans had tainted it. Love was connected with devotion, which made me think of God. God, who I didn't want to think about because I felt that was too big a topic for me to handle. Religion felt automatic at that point. I had fallen into a state of uncaring. Maria feared people had begun to believe love was about purity rather than passion, containment rather than flow, expectation rather than wonder. I had only my parents and my sister to view as examples. In time, Maria led me to see them as important connections I needed to maintain. Following this lesson, which was on a Monday, the day my sister and her husband bought their first mortgage and house, I gave her husband, Robert, one of Maria's gold nuggets. I'd never seen him so surprised. He asked me if I'd heard of Ballarat and offered to take me there. I offered the same trip to Maria.

Maria visited my home only once in a while, when neither of us wanted to be alone. We had my lessons at her house, usually—her new home in the Dandenong Ranges. I was the one who found it for her; my parents and I had a favourite café up there, and on the drive I would always wonder what those uphill driveways dug into the cliff-side led to.

Entering her property, one was immediately greeted by wrought iron-window grates painted white, already peeling to reveal the rust, and pot plants everywhere. There was a cow wandering among the trees in the backyard. Ants crawled up the wall in the kitchen in a single-file; two or three skittered across the dining table. She shooed them away whenever we ate. In Maria's house, there was always a solution. Shoo away the ants. Be kind to the cow, to have it produce milk. And when it stormed, pray to Maria, and she would bring back the sun.

I was sure the other homes in the ranges weren't like this.

After each lesson, I left her on her mountain with a promise to remember what I'd learned, and she left me another ginger root.

* * *

I began to pity Daniel the more he and Maria saw each other. Without her, Daniel felt tired. Life meant nothing without Maria. I couldn't tell if I was jealous or not. He was committed in a way I'd never seen before. Days without Maria felt like suffocation, he said. When he walked, his feet felt bruised by the asphalt. When he breathed, he smelled smoke and chemicals. After he met Maria, he began to seek the green in between the concrete. He told me how strange it was, to have the green background of his world suddenly mean everything. The green followed him wherever he went. In a fervour, he announced to Maria on their second meeting that he'd begun a garden of his own. She told him that was lovely. He told her he was obsessed. She told him that was lovely. She cleaned his room for him, and cooked him meals he found exotic. She whispered, she crooned: *kakainin kitang buhay.*[5] She put her hand on his lap. He grew under her kindness.

They saw each other once a week. Every time, she held onto his shoulder while she took off her shoes. And he still did not see the dirt on her feet. He bought her a gold chain and fastened it around her ankle, licking his thumb to scrub away the lines of blood down her legs. They grew intimate. He brushed her hair in the mornings and ignored the insects and spiders that

---

5   *kakainin kitang buhay:* 'I am going to eat you alive.'

burrowed in the black strands. He called her the light of his life. She said she loved him. He asked for her full name.

'Why?' she replied.

'Because I want to give you mine.' And he promised her a better future.

There was just one thing Daniel could never get the hang of. The Dandenong Ranges wasn't a far trip, but getting to Maria made all the difference. The mountain becomes hard to reach. Down the M1, it was easy to feel like your exit would never come. Up Stud Road, turn at Burwood Highway. Wondering how people could live so far from the comforts of dense shopping centres and suburbs. Here, there were trees and a grey asphalt road that never ended. That feeling of driving up a winding road you know will never end. But it became easier when I knew what I was driving to; the problem with Daniel was that he didn't.

Daniel worried about making his turns too fast, his eagerness pushing down on the accelerator. His stomach lurched when the car leaned too far right or left. And there was always something. A bird hitting his windshield. A short storm only for him. Branches curving over the road like teeth. He had never been comfortable among too many trees. He didn't like that they were taller than him, and he didn't like that he couldn't see through the forest.

He told me once that he preferred the sea, where his father had taken him out sailing as a child, and where his mother taught him how to swim. The sea was deep, but he could always count on the sun being on the horizon. The clear separation of sky and sea.

In the forest, he could count on nothing. It consumed him.

* * *

In those days, and in the days until I moved out, my parents were not comfortable with me coming home late. Eleven-forty-five was when I walked past the threshold one night, my stomach full from eating out, wiping my shoes on the welcome mat before kicking them off entirely, slipping my feet into my *tsinelas*.[6] Unlike Maria, I kept my feet clean. I picked off a

---

6   *tsinelas*: slippers, flip-flops.

spider from my shoulder and let it crawl up a wall. Eleven-forty-five meant everyone was usually getting around to sleep.

But the table that night was occupied by my father, eating a plate of *tinola* and rice, the smell of the ginger and the chicken soup wafting through the house. Peeking into the kitchen, I could see the cut pieces of green papaya bobbing up and down in the silver pot. The ginger reminded me of the new heaviness in my pocket, but I still prepared myself a plate and ate. No matter how I felt, I could always eat.

After my mother scolded me for eating so late, my father spoke to me as we both put our finished plates in the sink for washing.

'*Anak*, come help me after, ha,' he said.[7]

He was leaving again for the Philippines. He lives there permanently now, but back then he left often for work, or to check in on our family. I had to help him take the luggage down from the cabinets in my room. The task fell to me since my sister had moved out and my mother was too short. I asked him if I could come with him this time. It was tradition for him to say no. It was too busy, too crowded, too dirty, he explained, and it wouldn't be good for me. He added that this was why he brought us here. So that *nothing* would happen. As if I hadn't lived there for a few years, as if those years didn't count. As he spoke, I picked off another insect I felt crawling from behind my ear down my neck. Flicked it away.

In my room, my mother knocked on the door as she opened it, and she reminded me that tomorrow was Sunday. There was a priest from home coming, and it was very special. She insisted it was an opportunity for me to work on my Tagalog, then asked if I could please wear the nice white dress, *kung malinis na't wala nang dugo*,[8] and if not, the blue one was fine. I barely had time to think that my mother's idea of 'home' was different from my own now. I told her the white dress was clean.

The maya bird appeared when my mother left.[9]

'I'm going to church tomorrow morning,' I said. 'Will you come?'

---

7   *anak*: 'child'; *ha*: a commonly used exclamation, as if to say 'come help me after, okay?' but does not literally mean 'okay.' It is usually used to make a command feel more like a request.

8   *kung malinis na't wala nang dugo*: 'If it's clean and there's no more blood.'

9   Maya birds are small, common birds in the Philippines.

The bird asked if my parents had asked about Daniel yet. I said no. The bird came up to kiss me on the cheek. It reminded me to be devout. It told me it would try to make it.

* * *

Before Mount Dandenong, there was another mountain. We would drive past it, on the way to *Lola's* house in Quezon province. A five-hour trip. A van packed with my cousins from my mother's side. We see the mountain shaped like a woman. We stop at a restaurant (Rose and Grace, Santo Tomas, Batangas) and we convene and *Lola* begins her stories:

There's a *diwata* who lives there.[10] *Lola* advised us to leave the mountains alone, but if we had absolutely no choice, we had to thank the spirits for allowing us entry. Show respect always. When she was young, she and the girl scouts would go camping on the mountain and there would be a woman in white in the forest who greeted them. One night, the fairy told them who she really was: she wasn't a fairy at all, but a goddess. Her dress of pounded tree bark swapped for the virgin white. Her real name forgotten; 'Maria,' coming from a virgin woman different from herself. Like the Old Testament turned into the New, the vengeful God turned into a loving one. The last thing *Lola* told us was Maria's real name, whispered to her by Maria herself.

That Sunday, I watched three children fulfil their sacrament of confirmation. The priest from home had taken a step to the side, the snappy air of Tagalog switched back to the drawl of English, and the parish priest took centre-stage. The priest from home just smiled, nodding, as each child stated their new names. Joan, of St Joan of Arc. Matthew, of St Matthew, the Apostle. Mary, of St Mary Magdalene.

Joan's white dress was so beautiful, my mother tried to take out her disposable camera to take a picture of it. She knew her nieces would love something like that made for their confirmation. The dress glimmered in silk, a string of pearls around her neck.

---

10   *diwata*: a type of deity, or spirit, loosely similar to fairies or elves.

Matthew had blonde hair and blue eyes, which had all my aunts and the women around me smiling in approval as he stood next to Mary, the brown-haired, brown-eyed girl.

Mary, who, after the ceremony and the mass, ripped off the flower crown with the short veil on her head, who smudged her hand across her rouge-stained lips and it appeared as if blood streaked across her cheeks. When she smiled, her sharp, baby teeth were also stained with red. Mary, who I could so easily see as one of those children playing on a street in any *barangay*,[11] dressed in thinning clothes, drivers honking the horn to warn the children they were rushing past, in case they ran onto the road. She tugged on Joan's skirt, pointing out the group of children outside. Unbridled by their parents, the children gathered their suits and skirts and took off. Mary's feet left behind a trail on the blue carpet of the church.

I thought about how I had already forgotten my confirmation name, or at least my mouth didn't let me speak it. I could probably find it among my mother's old files. At the time, it never struck me how careless and confused it all was. When I was twelve, I was confirmed. I had a new name because it was just part of the process.

It was a secret name, one that I would never actually use and would never be known by. What was the use of something like that? My name is Nina. I hated having to explain the name given to me by my parents, no one here could tell if I was meant to be called both, or one or the other, so I chose for them.

I had come a long way with my name. Nina, from Maria-Nina, by my family who moved so that I would have a better future. Before that: *Maria ng Makiling*, Maria of the Mountain, from the place the people remember me most. The name became merged with Rizal's words: *Mariang Makiling*, the most beautiful, the most loving, and the most kind version of myself. And the first, like a first love, unforgettable with its lessons, and broken from me: *Diyan Masalanta*. Goddess of a land covered in the languages of other men. Wise protector of lovers, and of families. Pray to me for guidance, and to bring an end to storms.

---

11   *barangay*: a village, or suburb.

27

Counter Man

Carl Voller

'Are you counter man today, Carl?' Duty Sergeant Dalton asked me as he strode from his glass-cornered office. He seemed to brim with relief, knowing that despite universal hatred of the counter shift *I* hadn't 'gone sick.' He passed a glass wall bearing newspaper clips of police heroisms and black-and-white photos of a 1980 child-rape-murder arrest.

'Lady at the counter wants to report a traffic crash. Sounds like *the* job for you,' he said.

'Yep, that's for me.'

I thought: Dalton likes to rub it in; lazy individual—wouldn't take a report to save himself. I'll get hammered on the counter today—domestics, traffic crashes and every mentally-ill person on the coast will be in here. More paperwork is the last thing I need. How will I talk her out of a report?

I got some nice squeaks out of my boots on the lino floor as I strode to the front counter.

Waiting for me was Jean, with blue tresses. She had a strangely nonplussed look on her face.

'I wasn't going to report this, but I think it should go on record. I was hit by a car in the Valley yesterday evening.' She looked at me through the Perspex and I sensed she was serious, not crazy.

She was pleasant to look at, with kindly blue eyes and a country-English complexion—all topped with a lilting Scottish accent.

Any *injury* traffic crash needed a report, *especially* car versus pedestrian.

'Were you actually *hit* by the car?'

Her lips pursed and her eyes widened. I got the message clearly.

'Do you have *any* injuries?'

'Two small bruises on my right hip and thigh.'

So, out came the official police notebook, to take down some *uncomfortable* details.

'I went to the Brunswick Hotel with friends, after work,' she said. 'After drinks at the pub, we waited to cross Brunswick Street. My friends, three of them, crossed ahead of me, as I had trouble with the straps of my high-heels.'

'Yeeeess,' I said.

'I was trying to run and catch up to them in my new shoes.'

'Then?'

'I heard a roar like a racing-car engine to my right.'

'Where were you looking?'

'Toward my friends across the road.'

'Okay. Yes.'

'It happened quickly. I only had time to turn slightly to my right.'

'Then.'

'I remember bracing myself to be hit by a car and killed.'

'And.'

'The car hit me.'

'Describe the car?'

'Blue colour is *all* I can say. And I only noticed the blueness as it was driving away... in the distance.'

'The car *hit* you. Tell me about that?'

'Just as the car was right next to me, a big, blinding flash of white light came between me and it. It took nearly all of the impact. The car only spun me around and I lost balance.'

'Really! A blinding white flash of light?'

'Yes, and big.'

'What do you think it was—*an angel*?'

'No, no—just bright light.'

28

The Children of Monsters

Carl Voller

Your chin is resting awkwardly on your chest as a call blasts from the police radio at 4.49 in the morning. Street lights blaze through the windscreen. Your brain drags from auto-sleep mode, ending your dream at the part where the police-station door bumps against your heels: end-of-shift. Sleep flees, but it will not be long before the work is over, at least for another night.

This shift started at the police station at 10pm last night. That was when marked sedan, Sierra Charlie 454, peeled out of the driveway with you plumped in the passenger seat scratching job details on a clipboard. Your circadian rhythms are still staggering around the station hallway, searching for someone who looks like you.

A blazing set of eyes from childhood nightmares fixes upon you. Fear sprints through your veins. There's *something* in the night air. You sense it like a trained police dog. But constrained within your vehicle and your skin, you are blinded to such things.

'This one is a triple-O hang-up call, code 312, job number 347,' the radio operator informs. 'Domestic violence—proceed code three.'

You respond, 'Proceeding code three.'

With a flick of the steering wheel, Vince adds, 'We don't need it. We don't want a job like this. Not a domestic at *this* hour.'

You say, 'The *last* thing.'

You settle back in your seat, imagining the darkness you are about to walk into. Always the same. It's unnatural to walk willingly toward possible death. But that is what police do, with their weapons made-to-kill. The brave speak a common language, a gibberish on the border of courage and foolishness.

Courage or foolishness? Which is it for you, officers? Which one?

'Did it just get cold or is it me, Vince?'

'Think it's you, mate.'

You know he is lying. Ever the tough guy. It's 14 December 2014. Summer. Early but still dark. Someone has opened a fridge inside the car.

'Should we ask them if the seven o'clock crew can take it?'

'Why bother? Comms'll say no.'

'Hopefully there's nothing in it.'

'Where is this place anyway? There is no unit four, number 12 in this street. The numbers only go to eight. Or is it those units across the road near the shops? *Whatever.*'

'VKR, Sierra Charlie 454—show us off at this job.' The spiralled microphone cord twangs as you slam the mouthpiece into its dashboard holder. Vince raises an eyebrow. You leave the safety of Sierra Charlie 454 and shake away the seduction of sleep.

Time stutters, then stands still. An *apparition* prepares a welcome for *you*, deep within the bricks and mortar of the block. Its head is high above the ceiling, as it is with spiritual presences over ten feet tall. A foreign coldness invades the air.

Rays of sun touch palm leaves as your boots step up the incline of the concrete driveway. The units rear upwards into the sky like the hood of a cobra preparing to strike. The air draughts in the transition between light and dark. A presence glides smoothly, snake-like, into every gap in the building. The palm leaves rustle in a blast of wind.

Convince yourself there is nothing different about this job. Just another domestic. Another routine police job. They're all the same, aren't they?

You flick the switch of your hand-held radio, like so many times before. That back-and-forth whenever you leave or enter the police car. Like you, your audio recorder is awake, recording the sounds of the morning. Between brief silences, you hear dust shuffle. Sunrise hovers.

Your weapon rests in its thigh-holster. All fifteen hollow-pointed rounds in the Glock nine-millimetre are waiting to crash a hole through some undesirable's chest. Glock weaponry, designed by an Austrian curtain-rod maker for the killing of Australians. Each hollow-pointed round has DEATH written around its mouth in invisible ink. Outlawed by the Geneva Convention in times of war—but this is not (strictly speaking) war.

The Glock has a half-brother named Taser, who resides in the holster on the left side of your utility belt, resplendent in yellow and black. Taser rests just below your blue mesh load-bearing vest. The reverse-grip butt asserts its authority by shoving some palm leaves aside. Taser is also impatient to demonstrate action, in the form of *shock and awe* to any crims foolish enough to mess with you or your partner.

Even the inanimate seem alive. It is like the smell and energy in the air before a wild storm.

From the cool morning darkness within the unit block, a *monster* eyes your blue uniforms and scoffs. He can jam a pistol or Taser and render them useless by a mere thought. It may be the *time* for one of you brave police officers to pour out your blood, joining your fathers in the dust.

Another police funeral—the women in black with their hair gathered in ribbons. Their bare heels balance on shiny stilettos. The babies in pristine prams stare at the gathered angels, oblivious to the dress hems and pressed trousers. The angels look back into their eyes. In their own strange way, the innocents know more about this celebration of life and death than the adults.

But nothing happens—unless *the monster* wills it. *So he believes.*

You're in a domain that is not your own. You cannot see that there is a puppet-master nearby, one who can pull a copper's strings.

An abattoir killing-knife lays under a box on the floor of the upstairs bedroom. A scimitar that has cut the throats of countless squealing pigs. Its razor edge has opened rivers of blood.

And you are the latest *pig*-victim. You will scream like a terrified porker, your flapping hands trying to stop the life-blood gushing from your neck.

Why am I scared? And why do I feel like I am going to die? I feel so alone. Sick in the guts. I wish that I had taken the time *to say 'Sorry' to Belinda last night for what I did. Was it for lack of courage or lack of humility?*

Your eyes mist over with tears. Dwell alone in your weakness. You will always find yourself alone. There will be no comfort, not even from 100 of your partners-in-blue. No solace: your only friends will be 'loneliness' and your two beloved workmates who committed suicide.

I have never trusted Vince; not since those old rumours about him and my former wife. 'I would never do that mate,' he said, his stupid moustache smirking. Begged me to believe him. Nice-as-pie to my face—but I know him. He would stab me in the back as quick as look at me. Went through the academy together—26 years ago. The best of mates, but not anymore.

'That's unit two there. Hmmm, this is it here, unit four.'

You recall Belinda kissing you at 9:10pm, and her words linger: 'Be careful, I will always love you.' But *does she*, really? Then, you went off to 'cop-land.' Precious words from a policeman's wife. And her thoughts and prayers are to God. She will miss you when you're gone. You really do hate your policeman's life, don't you?

'You go first.'

A metallic 'tap-tap' resonates from the butt of your torch against the metal door frame.

No answer.

Can't see anyone inside yet, but have a strange feeling that someone or something is there *in that living room. A shadow, like the outline of a giant torso: the shoulders and head* gone, *lost beyond the ceiling.*

Your mind is in turmoil. Think you're going crazy.

The door is unlocked. You shuffle in. Your senses have something approaching cat-like awareness, your boots fumble on the tiled foyer. Block your mind from all thinking. Thinking is bad right now. Feel Vince's shaking hand as he brushes your shoulder. Ignore it.

Everything about this job is bad.

Fear is in your blood. Feel it coursing through you. But you are used to years of handling this type of fear, masking it with anger. Let anger and violence take over. Give of yourself. Let them take you where *they* want to go. Become *the monster.*

I've been thinking a lot about dying lately anyway. Better to die a hero's death. But I am ready to kick some serious butt first.

A voice. 'Who is it?'

You bark back 'Police' as a shirtless male wearing blue floral boardies bounces down the last few of the carpet-covered stairs. He hesitates.

His face is a play-actor's mask of feigned surprise and false concern. Your eyes meet and the moment stands still. What is under the mask? Don't trust him. Looks like he lied his way through the birth canal.

Caucasian male, fair complexion, 175 centimetres, muscular build, medium-length brown hair, eye colour—*who cares? What's his next move?*

He's about two metres away and closing.

'I know why you're here guys. I'll be getting kicked out. She's over there.'

Vince steps quickly to a patio and takes up with a 21-year-old female and a nine-month-old baby girl. Her face says bedraggled and forlorn. Her unrestrained floating breasts attempt to jump out of her loose dirty top. The kid is in a plastic baby-walker. She has curly brown hair. With clock-work regularity, the walker, with one wheel missing, is scraped on the concrete patio surface. Green vines wind around the timber pergola and mould has taken over the concrete below. Small multi-coloured kites dance from the upper parts of the frame. There's no roof and the morning sun illuminates the mother's awkwardness and embarrassment. The baby's arms embrace the walker.

Shirtless male's pockets are checked.

'Sit down and we'll talk. Can I see your ID?'

Co-operative. No weapons (that you can see). No aggro towards police—he must have vented on her. You scan him up and down, anticipating something out-of-control happening.

Vince appears to be scribbling something in his notebook while he's getting an earful from *her*. He's getting pissed off with the kid. Vince has never married, never had kids. Never will.

The 'baddie' doesn't want to say anything. Fine, for now.

He is too *good. About to try something on. Will he jump up in the next second and grab me by the throat or something? Not drunk or 'off his face.' Why isn't he abusing us, or at the least, being a smart alec?*

I allow him to go to the doorway and inhale his precious cigarette. I wait. Try to suck clean air from the opposite direction. Watch her too—head bopping and arms waving as she talks to Vince. Vince is wearing his best Easter-Island-statue face. Just the facts ma'am.

I think of Belinda taking her bra off and turning her back on me. So I couldn't even look at her breasts. I'll never forget that. Making me feel like a stranger in my own bedroom. How could she do that to me? Be so cold. I can't touch her any more—now I'm not allowed to look at her. Why?

Shirtless male in blue floral boardies is wearing his false-remorseful face and he is *thinking*. He is a police-hater. You know it. For some *strange* reason he is not trying to argue with, even out-muscle, us.

Unbeknown to you, the fire in the monster's eyes has been quenched. And it's all because of the two figures standing behind *you*. They cannot be seen with mortal eyes.

Two dazzling guardian angels—princes of the host of Heaven, stand eye-to-eye with the monster—their gaze searing him, freezing him with dread.

Her allegations are briefly outlined to her partner, *your baddie*.

You say, 'She states that she was punched twice in the stomach while feeding the baby, and then you followed her into another room and choked her while your little girl played with toys on the floor. She says that her screaming caused your little girl to cry also.'

He says, 'Just go with what she says, boss. Nothin' I'm gonna say will make any difference.'

A handcuff snaps while you say, 'You are now under arrest for breaching a domestic-violence protection order.' Shirtless male co-operates by moving his other arm behind his back.

You watch her sad stare as she holds the baby close with one arm. She watches you lead the shirtless male away. You place a reassuring arm around his shoulder and sit him down in the back of the car.

Somehow, you feel sorry for him. That's what police call being *warm and fuzzy*. He lost control in a haze of anger and became his own monster, drawn into a storm of his own making. He drank from the cup of anger offered him by his *monster* companion. Someone else took control of him and he became *different*—two people in one. One is a monster.

You *do* feel sorry for him. You can see yourself in him. From dealing daily with monsters, you have become one. You have become a *monster* too. All that you have seen and done in your suit of blue has left you just as damaged and angry as *them*.

You are unable to go home and relax and play with your children, take your wife out somewhere nice. Instead, you are an irritable, short-tempered version of the kind and gentle man that you always strived to be. You are difficult to live with. Your temper is violent. Your family don't live with you, they endure you—and only because for some deep reason they love you.

Or do they?

Don't know why they do? If they do. Why?

You feel sorry for *him*.

You are a monster too.

The two versions of *him*—one with blazing eyes—sit together inside the watchhouse's concrete cell. One stares into the other's tear-washed face.

The morning sun blinds your vision. As always, two unseen princes of Heaven follow. The police station door eases behind you. Seven-fifteen. Shift's end.

Beware that, when fighting monsters, you yourself do not become a monster...
for when you gaze long into the abyss, the abyss gazes also into you.
– Friedrich Nietzsche

29

The Ripper

Michael Walton

The bushes that night were as dark as the sins they concealed. The streetlamps dripped cones of sodium light along the footpath; but – this light never dared to venture into Hyde Park. The moon was a silver sickle cutting a starless, godless dark. A dog whimpered pitifully, scratching at the door holding it back.

It was on this night that I became infamous, and it is the only night which I regret. My dear jurors, perhaps you have already equated me with the monsters that children imagine are stalking the dark. A thing, an enemy, an 'other': with curled horns and cloven hooves. A danger to you and your suburban picket paradise. A silhouette, haunting the streets by lamplight. Maybe you think that you too have seen me.

Perhaps you have. It is not unlikely. I passed some graffiti that night, scrawled sideways on a wall of bricks above heaped rubbish. I had to step over a woman, passed out and curled up on the pavement, her head between her legs. Her pants were stained with dark patches of defecation that turned my stomach. There was a thin line of translucent vomit shining over her cherry red lips. Above her, on the crumbling brickwork, a scrawl of angry red demanded.

Hang the Ripper.

Hang me, you kill only the body. I don't imagine it would be worth the rope. In every way that counts, I am already dead: remember that when you brood on my fate. There is still blood in my veins, a heartbeat in my breast, but that is all. Even as I write to you, it occurs to me that the sharp tip of this pen might be sufficient to puncture the web of pulsing blue veins I see in my wrist. But of course, that is not your concern.

Elaine MacDonald was sixteen when she was murdered. I could tell you she was a good girl, but that would be a lie. I could tell you she was always joyous and kind, but that too, would be a lie. I could tell you that she was one of the under-sixteen dance finalists and that when she was on stage she relished seeing the men in the audience shifting to hide her effect on them from their wives. Which one, dear jurors, do you think is true?

She was visiting her grandparents on that night. She always saw them after school on a Friday, except during the holidays when she could come any time. Her grandmother made tea, Earl Grey in a silver kettle that was a wedding present, while Elaine complained about her homework, her friends, and her dance shoes. The tea came in and contented her, then her grandfather cleared his throat. He left his tea untouched and asked her what she thought of the Ripper killings.

It took her a moment to gather her thoughts and in that single moment, her grandfather saw fear twist her features. Then she said she didn't know what to think. She said three dead prostitutes didn't make 'a Ripper' and that I was no Jack. She said that the media were playing it up to sell papers.

Her grandfather didn't like this, and she could tell, but she kept at it anyway: determined to have her say. She said that people were murdered all the time. She believed that they shouldn't report the murders: deny the killer the satisfaction of causing fear. In this way, she was like you: she didn't understand.

It was never about fear. I left my apartment about the same time Elaine's grandmother brought the tea through. I needed to go to the store to get some milk. There was only a rotting lettuce and a few moulding carrots in my fridge, not enough milk even for coffee. I trudged towards the store, along an empty road, as empty as a church on a weekday. I fell into its halo of lights and looked in on shelves piled high with boxes and jars. I did nothing more than glance, as my feet carried me on.

I passed the store.

I didn't stop.

Doubtlessly, my dear jurors, you have never been in such a position. Perhaps you have been distraught and perhaps you have been depressed, but I don't imagine you have felt as I did that night. If you did, you wouldn't be reading this. My life, and all the associated pressure and responsibility just fell away like footprints washed clean on the sand.

Elaine's grandfather sipped his tea before he spoke. He set his cup down, shifted uncomfortably and then admitted he thought they should bring back capital punishment for those like the Ripper. He began to speak very quickly then, his gestures growing erratic and firm. *A short drop and a sudden stop—* let them all swing!

Elaine started to object but her grandfather rushed over her, saying it should only be for the evil people, the broken people. People, he said, who did things of which even devils dare not dream: *people like this Ripper fella.* The ones who can't be fixed.

Elaine demanded to know who would have that power. Who was beyond saving? Who was so broken that the only solution was death? No one was beyond saving, she claimed, with a resolution that shamed her grandfather's. Unlike many who assert such things, she believed it. She believed it right up until the end. In that, she was extraordinary.

They had dinner around a small table draped in floral plastic. Roast chicken and vegetables served on the best china. Another pot of Earl Grey tea followed with a store-bought cake for dessert, cut with smiles and politeness. The Ripper wasn't mentioned again.

Elaine thanked them for dinner, hugged them and kissed both their cheeks. She said she wanted to walk home, arguing that it was only a few blocks and she needed the exercise. She claimed light-heartedly that her grandmother made her eat too much and she needed to walk it off. Her grandmother shook her head, said she was too thin anyway, but let her go. I imagine that moment haunts her.

She zipped up her boots, smiled once more to her grandparents and told them she would be back next week. Her grandfather apologised for not being able to walk her home: his bad knee was played up again. She smiled and squeezed his hand: *I will be ok,* she assured him.

I hear those words every night.

Hands in pockets, cold air making her lungs ache, Elaine walked the wide, sodium-lit streets. She walked with her head up, and eyes on the dark ahead. She walked with her fingers wrapped around the ridges of her keys. These are details that were absent from the newspapers.

Her breath misted, her muscles were glad to be moving. She couldn't believe that her grandfather believed in executing criminals. What had he called them? Broken people. She scoffed even at the memory of this. Who wasn't broken?

She kicked a piece of shattered brick. It clattered along the pavement, the sharp rattle breaking the stillness of the night. She heaved in another breath, her toe throbbing, shoulders knotted with tension. She waited for the echo of the sound to fade—frowning as she heard it carried on down distant streets.

Didn't she know? Things, once broken, are never the same. Silence could settle again in that street, but it would be a different kind of silence. Different, like a bone set after breaking, or a shattered window then taped to keep out the wind. Made whole but never the same. Just like people. She and I were not so different.

You are all broken, my dear jurors—what was that I heard? Shouted objections, wrinkled noses and raised eyebrows. Of course, you don't believe me. But I don't need to convince you. You can't have an opinion about a fact, contrary to political wisdom. Here, let me prove it to you. We will all die. Now, what's your opinion? Shout all you like but it doesn't matter, for it will happen. *As I am so shall you be, for I was as you are.*

Elaine lived across the road from Hyde Park. A quiet space usually reserved for young children to play, but also somewhat of a haven for prostitutes. It is tragic, desperately tragic, the way the innocent and the guilty intersect and occupy the same space, sharing the same air. I was angry at them once, for the waste of their lives. Maybe you are too. But I soon learned not to be angry with the rain; it simply does not know how to fall upwards.

The bushes are dark there and it is the cheapest place to have a prostitute. They gathered under the streetlamps, washed out and pale. Their lipstick was sloppy; they shivered under too-thin cardigans draped over too-little clothing. Their nipples stood erect against the night. Some of them were friends of Elaine, a few of them had been her classmates.

She walked over to them, hugged them, and smiled. They lit cigarettes in the cradle of their hands, and the ember tips glowed in the shadows. Like hope amid despair. Or the innocents among the guilty. Her mistake was to share space with them, her mistake was to breathe their air.

I have only one thing that I regret, my dear, damming, judges, and that is her. She had possibility in her life; she had not yet fallen into the same trap as the rest of you. A human life is an infinity of possibility, as are all the possible fractions between two and one.

How then does such vast possibility become the same damnable and mundane patterns, time and time again? Answer me this, if you will answer nothing else. Daughters become their mothers and sons their fathers. The victim becomes the perpetrator, whose victim then becomes the next and so on until there is no one left to hurt.

Life is a wheel, so is its violence. Over and over and over again it turns, crushing, grinding. Rising only to fall—like Lucifer raised to glory only to fall in fire, or the stars born only to collapse in violence. The wheel breaks a person, then moulds them into something they were not. All of you—hypocritical accusers!—are broken by this wheel.

Perhaps the psychologist has already given you a report on me: thick paper bound in a cream folder telling you I was attracted to my father. Or maybe that I had a bad experience with a prostitute, or maybe that I was a prostitute. They will talk about illness, trauma and disorder, using long words to say nothing at all.

They will rationalise me for you—pretend I can be reduced to something simple yet unknown—just not yet understood. And it will make you feel safe, to put a box around me, stick a label on and decide that's why I did it. Do you feel any better now?

Your psychologists will lie to you because I lied to them. It's a game of mine, like giving a child a piece of paper and crayons just to see what they come up with. Ignore them and make your own judgement.

Walk down the street and look about you. See the people there. The nice man who hands you your coffee. The woman walking a dog who smiles at you. The commuters who press against you on your way to work, yellowing newspapers open in their laps, rustling like leaves on a blustery autumn day. See their absent smiles which tell you they are harmless—you can trust them. They're just like you.

See them. And ask yourself, how well do you know them? Any could be a killer. Any could be a paedophile or a rapist. Why, then, do you trust them? Trust them not to pull you down an alley. Trust them not to hurt your children. Trust them to obey the law, the order, the social hypocrisy. How do you sleep at night?

The Answer: You have to pretend there is something different about me, something that makes me violent and dangerous, and not at all like them. That's why you have your cream folders, your degrees and your psychologists, isn't it? So, you can find a classification for me.

A set of criteria by which you can label, judge and detain. Based on this, you decide who lives and who dies. All of you are like docile pets who have learned to love your cage: love it so much that any thought of removing it, of daring to think for yourselves, sends you cowering to the corner.

That's why I did it, don't you see? Break the cages and let them be free. It's a sweet gift, freedom, but not one that everyone can manage on their own. Elaine could though, and that's my greatest regret. Not her death as such but robbing her of the chance to claim her freedom on her own. She would've been right beside me given half the chance: I know she would.

30

The Silk Hook

Aileen Westbrook

WINNER OF THE
MONASH UNDERGRADUATE PRIZE
FOR CREATIVE WRITING

When Evie recalled those sapling days of chubby infants, she gasped at her temerity. What ardour it takes to care for our young! Did Rilke not say, *to love another human being is the most difficult of our tasks, the work for which all other work is but preparation?* Perhaps every mother feels thus. Preparation: a daily ritual. Folding knapsacks, hats, girls, sox, tiny teddies into a car. Tenderness at the kiss and ride spot. Bypassing police vans lurking around corners on the lookout for child-killers clocking 60 in a 40 zone—Evie spared them the pleasure.

Now that she had her new office space, her 'salon' as she called it, Evie scarcely knew her other self. A boutique niche in an otherwise austere block in the Centre. From the outside, just another powder blue door in a corridor. The lino had an antiseptic gloss almost holy in its purity. Overhead fluorescent lights stripped you bare as a body search. But inside—bliss—

minimalist décor of dove grey walls tiered with IKEA shelves—perfect for her purposes. Everything in the Centre had a silvery cast—concrete benches, fretwork of balconies, the argent teeth of circumstance. Even her clients' skin had a soft, metallic tincture. A signature of sorts.

Evie held her breath in anticipation. Thursdays and Fridays were always manic. Her apprentice was in absentia, seconded to TAFE. Never mind: her clients would be greeted at the door by Security (there was a silver bell) and Evie wore her wrap-around apron, bottle-green with ties. Rather like a kimono, but cotton.

Evie relished a few minutes of solitude before her first appointment of the day. There they were, her conspirators: hundreds of them lined-up on the shelves in their coiffed glory. Strawberry, copper, honey, jet, butterscotch, mulberry, liquorice and ash. Of course, all were beheaded. So to speak. There was Marie-Antoinette at the end—bouffant with rosebud lips. Next was Cate Blanchett—serene as chamomile. Evie sighed at Cate's tresses and twitched a stray wisp from her nose. *Who shall I be this morning?* she asked her silent companions. Evie untied her scarf and ran a hand over her smooth scalp. Sliding Cate's wig off her waxy head, Evie pulled it snugly over her own. One of the felicities of the job. The bell buzzed, tizzy as a blow fly in a bell jar. Evie opened her drawer of tricks, reaching for a comb, clips, a crochet hook. She bowed to her be-wigged friends and greeted her first client of the day.

Claudia—good morning! Evie held out her hand to an emaciated woman with bruised eyes. *Now, don't cry. Come, sit here. Yes, in front of the mirror. Here's a tissue. Now, let's look at you.* Claudia was so thin that her green tunic gaped like a surgical gown. *The chemo was tough, wasn't it? But hark this—hair is simply modified skin—it sheds—it returns. Now, I can see from your eyebrows, those soft hairs on your arms, your freckles: you were a titian goddess. Let's see what magic I can weave.*

Evie circled her client, tilting her head, pursing her lips, observing Claudia's dappled cheeks, beaked nose, valiant chin. She placed her hands, gentle as moth wings, on Claudia's temples. *A wig-maker requires patience, delicacy, strong hands. These qualities I have, Claudia. I crochet my wigs by hand, so that the hair cascades as a waterfall. No matter how it is parted.*

This tape measure might be a little cold on your scalp... Forgive me! 26 centimetres. Let me jot that down. Now, don't mind my supervisor hovering, Claudia, Evie murmured softly, nodding towards a female in a no-nonsense gunmetal blue shirt who had entered the room, rubber soles squeaking on the lino. *Of course, I had another life before wig-making,* chatted Evie in gentle distraction. *My mother had aspirations for me to be a Marie Curie— or a Rosalind Franklin—so I pursued chemistry with daughterly fervour. Dwelt among protein chains and polypeptides. Deciphered nucleotides of telomeres—little protective caps on the ends of your chromosomes Claudia—like plastic tips on school shoelaces. Alas, if your telomeres are short, you die young!* Evie sighed.

Then I met my husband. Karl. An exchange student besotted with Rilke— and me—for a time. Before the circus began! We had three little girls—a brood! Damask, Tabby and Organza. A triple miracle, all germinated from eggs in a test-tube. And you Claudia?

Two boys, sniffed Claudia, weepy again. *Tim and Harry, grown up now. They never visit me here.*

O Boys! Short-back-and-sides, soothed Evie. *How fate chases us. All my girls had long plaits—shading from flaxen to mouse-brown—I used to hoard their pigtails after trimming. In labelled bags. Zip-locked. Imagine, a chest of plaits. A reliquary of sorts!*

That's the virtue of hair, isn't it? inquired Claudia anxiously, touching her downy patches of re-growth. *It grows perpetually, doesn't it, like fingernails?* She looked to Evie for reassurance. *Even after death?*

Evie paused, her tape measure springing out like an uncoiling snake of chromatin. True, hair was an exceedingly stable, triple-layered microfibrillar structure which resisted decomposition for thousands of years. This thought had long consoled Evie. Yet at stray moments, Evie was seized with disquiet. The high walls seemed to reproach her where the paint peeled off like flailed skin. Blue graffiti, insects of biro scribble, crawled in corners. The testimonies of banished souls.

Evie marshalled herself. Should she counsel Claudia on the cycle of growth and decay? *Only last week I saw two clients whose hair had been yanked* *out—during random scuffles or some such—*confided Evie. *Great clumps—like kikuyu grass ripped from a nature strip. But I excel at reviving the lost! You see, hair is rejuvenant by nature,* Evie continued, her tape measure circumnavigating Claudia's skull. *For instance, my girls' plaits just kept growing, and I kept filing them away in colour-coded trays.* Evie paused in memory of the rows of plaits sleeping side-by-side in the sandalwood-scented chest. *As for post-mortem growth—it is theoretically possible,* Evie said wrinkling her brow, *if there's a little residual glucose in the bloodstream. I'm hardly an expert—I suppose there are cadaver studies.*

Evie's tape measure slithered to the floor as she fell into reverie. Muffled voices, a quarrel outside, roused her. Evie put a hand on Claudia's bony shoulder. *Don't fret,* she whispered, *it's the new woman down the hall—Harriet—a bit resistant to the rules of the Centre. Now where was I...? My personal experience of hair is perhaps singular, Claudia. Harrowing, even. My father called me his magpie—apt—for I've always had a fondness for collecting nature's curios (cicada wings, carpet beetles, kittens' milk teeth). And I was black-winged as a magpie. Until that night, Claudia. I still shudder to think of the fate of my black ponytail.* Evie closed her eyes and rubbed the nape of her neck.

It was the night Karl submitted his dissertation on Rilke's angels. I woke to something slithery writhing on my pillow—squid black skeins of my forsaken hair! A Greek threnody of sorrowful strands abandoned by my body. 'Why?' my borderline hysterical husband demanded of doctors who pored over my idiopathic follicular chemistry. 'Perhaps stress of an inflammatory kind,' they surmised, grasping at diagnostic straws.

It took three days, Evie recalled solemnly. *A shedding of black threads till I was completely shriven. I held vigil at my own wake. Bereft, I sobbed when my daughters hid inside their wardrobe. I had to coax them out wearing a mink hat.*

> I am a bear I growled
> from Antarctica
> where bears lose their fur coats in wintertime
> (I fibbed—they were small)
> A rite of hibernation I soothed
> (what you do for love)
> It was my husband who proposed a wig
> before he left

It's the revenge of the Gods I wailed
recalling Barbies I'd ravaged on the veranda under the scribbly barks
scissored fronds of hair sailing off
a flotilla of blonde stamens in a eucalypt haze
but I now see it all began unravelling with Mrs Frew's eggs.

Claudia, how are you? Did you hear that ruckus last night—screaming from C block—and then the sirens? I suspect it was a cache of illicit substances, Evie said sotto voce, *stuffed in a tennis ball. Drugs, they shorten your telomeres, you know, damage the nucleotides.*

Perhaps it was that new girl, Harriet, hissed Claudia, while the supervisor fiddled with her radio in a corner of the room. Evie raised a conspiratorial eyebrow and waved her comb. *Now, let's put those in-house dramas aside— take a seat. Pop your feet on the footstool. I have been crocheting a silk cap for your wig.* She placed the bonnet on Claudia's head. *Perfect,* pronounced Evie, clapping. *Now to select a hairstyle. Then I can begin threading hairs through the eyelets. Human hair is best.* Evie flourished a crochet hook—a sleek silver instrument. *A bob, or curls?* Evie perused her shelves. *Would you consider Miranda Otto? Flowing yet demure. There's always my Silverwater Beauty—the name is befitting, don't you think? I like to imagine we can hear the swelling tide of the Parramatta River—just a stone's throw away really—if we clambered up onto the roof! O you're tempted by my Outlander, Claire? (So timeless.) I wonder if she might be a little dark for your complexion? Come, let's see…*

An hour later, Evie was smoothing the tresses of Nicole Kidman over Claudia's shoulders. *Apricot silk,* she murmured. *Now, Claudia, where was I in my life cycle? Yes, it was a teaspoon of silkworm eggs that threw me. Spawn of the domesticated silkworm 'Bombyx mori.'* Even now, Evie remembered that seemingly ordinary school day. *Mrs Frew says that's all they eat,* Tabby had insisted, yellow plaits bouncing in the car seat. *Leaves of the black mulberry tree. Their life cycle depends on it,* Tabby had lisped through a paddle-pop.

It was a descent into devotion that only mothers bear, Evie confided to Claudia. *That night, and nights to follow, I scoured the streets for 'Morus nigra.' Even Miranda next door was in the same plight, our lives at the mercy of tiny glinting mouths. Mouths that plundered kilos of illegally plucked verdure. O the furore! The ceaseless chomping! Five times, the silver worms shed their skins like worn-out masks. And at the brink of each unmasking, the pupa would raise its head in wonderment, as if in an act of prayer. O Claudia, when the feeding ceased, I wept. I slept. For in all those weeks, Claudia, my head scarcely touched a pillow. Perhaps it's a flaw in my nature. I neglect the quotidian for the quest. I've always been one to go down rabbit burrows searching for...*

Evie paused, collapsing on the grey plastic bench, one hand to her brow, bewildered. What *had* she been chasing?

On those midnight vigils, she'd crawled on all fours seeking vagrant silkworms. 'Wanderlings,' she'd called them in her mind. Snug in boxes for weeks, stuffing their alimentary canals with leaves until: *The Call.* Silver worms on a mission. They'd migrate to foreign corners—seeking crevices to spin cocoons. Evie would nap on the floorboards with one eye open, a magnifying glass squashing her lashes, mesmerised by silk threads oozing from spinnerets, while silkworm bodies rotated in a figure-of-eight dance, encasing themselves in a silk tomb. A waltz of infinity. The *ouroboros* of life.

Feeling dizzy, Evie ushered Claudia through her blue door, disclosing a factual nugget even David Attenborough might applaud. *They never fly, Claudia, the moths, once they hatch. A completely domesticated species. They never leave the nest.*

How is your wig after your first month, Claudia? It's not washing well? Limp? I'll soak the fibres in an almond bath. O! I spy some ginger fuzz on your scalp—a meadow of growing tips. Excellent! Now, your diet? Nuts are vital for stimulating follicles. Just relax while I massage emu oil into your roots. Claudia moaned in pleasure while Evie's fingers traced small circles on her scalp. *How lucky you are to have your hair salon service Evie,* murmured Claudia. *When I'm well, I'll*

have to return to the bakery in E block. I suppose that's better than laundry. Or untangling Qantas head-sets.

Claudia, I confess baking has never been my forte, replied Evie, ever honest. *After Karl left, I felt a little overwhelmed with so many small mouths to feed. My girls were always picky eaters. Sausages, a blessing! Kebabs! Tidbits you could throw under the griller. Especially when I had to spend evenings cruising the neighbourhood for mulberry trees. What can you do when all specimens in a five kilometre radius of the school are denuded? When I finally spotted one outside the bottle shop—viridian in splendour—I tore leaves from its limbs and stuffed them into a black draw-string bag like a woman demented. Triumphant—I staggered home—threw the girls in front of Harry Potter with their sausages, and dispensed leaves to the voracious silkworms.*

Then, one morning I was sipping my tea. Plop! A golden cocoon fell into my cup. Buoyant as a yellow floatie. Just as foretold in the legend of Lei-Tse, wife of the Yellow Emperor in ancient China. It was a sign, Claudia! If an empress could invent silk looms and grow silkworms on her mulberry farm, I could do it in my own dining room. Did not Voltaire say, 'We must cultivate our own garden'? At first, the girls helped chopping leaves, clearing frass (that's silkworm poo) from the clogged boxes, but you know small children. They get bored, retreat to their cubby houses. Yet with so many mouths to feed, what could I do? Verily, it was a labour of love, but it took its toll.

Once the feeding phases ceased, Claudia, I could catch my breath. I spent whole afternoons observing larval activities. I salvaged my old microscope, made serial sections of pupating specimens on the kitchen counter. After a few weeks I had fully documented their life-cycle in sequential drawings. (I borrowed Tabby's Derwent pencils and she helped colour the wingtips.)

But you know how it is when children start feeling neglected, Claudia? It was as if their umbilical cords were still tugging. 'What's for dinner?' Organza would ask, burrowing into my lap. 'Oh darling, mummy's busy.' Tabby would pluck at my hem as I climbed ladders to inspect cocoons lodged steeple-high. Damask would drag her mermaid tail through the dust bunnies on floor, begging for some Jatz. 'Let's see what's on the menu,' I replied, surveying the fridge. A pallid lettuce. Nutella. A shrivelled pot of nasi goreng. Shelves of freezer bags stuffed with mulberry leaves. 'Let's do noodles,' I said.

I was cross when the Department of Education came knocking one afternoon complaining that the girls were skipping school. 'So naughty,' I murmured, smiling regretfully, my boot jammed in the door, willing them to go. The hall was havoc, Claudia, thousands of gold cocoons dangling from miniature silk ropes, a fecund smell of copulation wafting from the dining room. 'Girls,' I called, beckoning my shy guinea pigs. 'They're playing in the garden,' I told the visitors, raising my eyes to heaven with a mother's knowingness. 'Their attendance rate simply must improve,' was the icy admonishment. After the inspectors left, I tried to calm myself. Perhaps I should have a tête-à-tête with my tender tribe. Check homework, zip through times-tables. I poked my head into the girls' bedroom, spying three small mounds under Damask's doona. My chrysalid children in their silk womb. I let them sleep. The rest is lost in a miasma of days—for I had new generations of silkworms hatching—so many mouths to feed.

I look to the Wheel of Fortune, Rota Fortunae, Claudia. If Mrs Frew hadn't given Tabby those eggs that day—all part of the kindergarten Life-Cycle-Awareness Program—I'd probably still be counting sox and doing the school drill. I wouldn't be in my salon, if it wasn't for the domestic flight path that brought me here.

Offspring—they're a gift and a heart-ache, pronounced Evie as she skewered Claudia's curls in a French twist. *What did Rilke say? 'Love: the last test and proof.' And yet... he abandoned his own baby daughter.* Disconcerted by the eccentric orbit of such logic, Evie went to her desk. *Claudia, have I shown you a snap of my girls? My triple joys?* Evie nursed a small gilt-frame in her hands. *Tabby is the one in the middle. My spring babies... They would have been 30 next week.*

I brood about the nature of justice, Evie confessed, *combing Claudia's fringe vigorously. The judge said I hadn't mourned, shown any remorse.* 'That's not true,' I said, showing him the evidence: the wig I'd woven from the girls' plaits. (It was a sort of Rococo, Neo-Victorian concoction, Claudia. Soft blonde and caramel ropes, pinned in roundels over the ears.) 'David Attenborough would have understood,' I shouted to the horrid judge in his horsehair wig. 'What do you know of the cosmic burden of motherhood?' Evie's words were clogged with tears.

Claudia passed Evie a tissue.

Now, Claudia dear friend, let's book you in for a month. Before you begin at the bakery. Perhaps we could try a citron summer look? Evie ushered Claudia to the door and Security (so absurdly stringent here) marched her client down the narrow corridor.

The final bell of the day was like a child's keening cry. Lock up time. Quickly Evie collected her tools, slipped off her wig and untied her kimono apron. The afternoon light fell slantwise from a high barred window, the razor wire beyond casting a ferny pattern over Evie's head. She thought of her spartan cell awaiting with its silver toilet seat and narrow bed. *O Rilke, how wrong you were to say we cannot cling to the dead*, whispered Evie. She burrowed her hand behind the rows of mannequin heads, searching. There it was, a vanilla-scented wig. She buried her face in its elaborately plaited whirls. *O my darlings, sleep tight.*

Acknowledgements

I am most grateful to Monash University for the opportunity to participate in a mentorship program offered through *Verge*. My sincere thanks to the editorial team at *Verge*, especially Calvin Fung, for generous guidance and encouragement.

31

Small Pebble

Gavin Yates

Swallow the rhubarb of rhubarbs—of random plain dirt. Lobby around
a nauseous head. The small requests; the smooth lines. Whole peninsulas,
tattered cloth, lattice. Mountaineering seams. Fade.

Contributors

Editors

Stephen Downes was this year awarded a PhD in creative writing from Monash University. His thesis investigates the influence of the uncanny and nostalgia on the prose fictions of the German writer W. G. Sebald. He has published some dozen non-fiction books, and a few have won prizes and been translated. His short story 'Anniversary' was selected for the UNESCO Cities of Literature anthology *A Tale of Four Cities*. Also a short story, 'The Sausage Caper' was shortlisted for the 2018 British Bridport Short Story Prize.

Calvin Fung likes to think his passion for Gothic literature is what strong-armed the other editors into agreeing with the theme of the uncanny for this year's *Verge*. He is in his second year of his creative writing PhD on Hong Kong Gothic literature. He was the highest-placed Monash University entrant of the 2017 Monash Prize. He is co-editor-in-chief of *Colloquy: Text, Theory, Critique*.

Amaryllis Gacioppo is an Australian writer. Recently she completed a joint PhD in creative writing with Monash University and the University of Bologna. In 2015 her story 'Dreams' won the Lord Mayor of Melbourne Award for Short Story. She has been shortlisted for various awards, including the Bristol Short Story Prize and the Scribe Nonfiction Prize. Her stories and essays have appeared in publications across Australia, the UK and the US.

Authors

Liz Allan is a PhD candidate in creative writing at The University of Adelaide and she runs The Adelaide Writers' Group. Liz was awarded the Rachel Funari Prize for fiction in 2018 and has been shortlisted for the Alan Marshall Short Story Prize and the Aesthetica Creative Writing Award. Her fiction has appeared in *Overland, Yen Magazine, Aesthetica* and *Best Summer Stories*.

Clancy Balen is a student at Monash University, currently completing a Bachelor of Arts with a minor in literature.

Grace Chan is mostly from Melbourne and works in mental health. She spends a large part of her time thinking about where people come from and where we're all going. Her passions include coffee, space operas, and increasing the diversity of speculative fiction. She has been published in *Going Down Swinging*. Her speculative-fiction novella *The Ship of Theseus* has been shortlisted for *Viva la Novella VII*.

Yvonne Deering has studied anthropology, English, education, art and design, as well as writing and editing. She lives in Central Victoria and has worked as a secretary, secondary and tertiary teacher, cleaner, dishwasher and waitress (in that order). Her writing draws largely on nature and place.

Ben Downes is a Melbourne gardener and the host of Travelman Podcast. His writing is influenced by the stories of J. G. Ballard, H. P. Lovecraft and Stephen King.

Jane Downing has had prose and poetry published in journals including *Griffith Review, Island, Southerly, Westerly, Overland, The Big Issue* and *Best Australian Poems* 2004 and 2015. Her two novels—*The Trickster* (2003) and *The Lost Tribe* (2005)—were published by Pandanus Books at the Australian National University. She has a Doctor of Creative Arts degree from the University of Technology, Sydney, and she can be found at http://www.janedowning.wordpress.com.

Natalie Evans is a medical student at Monash University. She has contributed to *The Doctus Project* and *GP First* magazine. In 2018 she placed second in the adult category of the Monash WordFest short-story competition and third in the open short-story category of the Boroondara Literary Awards.

Louise Falconer is a writer based in Castlemaine, Victoria. She has published extensively online as Weezelle@wordsandleaves and she reviews books for *Good Reading Magazine*. She has been published in *Underground Writers*, *Law/Text/Culture* and *Amida: The Asia Magazine*. In 2018 she was highly commended in the 2018 Writers Victoria Write-ability Fellowships. She is addicted to tea and is a penguin tragic.

Travis Franks is an RMIT creative writing graduate on the cusp of an Honours year. He has a penchant for weird fiction with a hint of melancholy and was shortlisted for the Monash Undergraduate Creative Writing Prize in 2017. He experiments with the recorded spoken word and his video prose has been published for Melbourne Knowledge Week.

Catherine Gillard lives in Fremantle, Western Australia. Her historical fiction manuscript, *The Incidental Nazi (The Choirmaster)*, was shortlisted for the TAG Hungerford Award in 2016. It is a fictionalised account of the Vienna Mozart Boys Choir's exile in Australia during World War Two and chronicles their fall from celebrity status to suspect aliens. She has self-published an historical fiction trilogy inspired by the life of Australia's first police woman. She has been published in UWA's literary magazine, *Westerly*. Catherine has a Master of Arts (Creative Writing) from UWA and will begin a PhD in Creative Writing in 2019. She is in her second year of a teaching fellowship in English and Literary Studies at the University of Western Australia.

Lauren Hay is nearing the end of a professional and creative writing degree at Deakin University. At poetry slams she has won and placed, and she was once a guest festival poet. She is revising her second novel and relishes reading about and writing characters who question themselves and their experiences. She would love her words to make readers think about things in new ways.

Suzanne Hermanoczki is a writer and teacher of creative writing. Winner of the *Affirm Press Creative Writing Prize* in 2014, her work which features migrants, bi-cultural identity, code-switching and multiculturalism, has been published in both local and international publications. She has a PhD in Creative Writing from the University of Melbourne, where she currently teaches.

Reanna Kissell is a current postgraduate student at Monash University studying librarianship and archives. She holds a Bachelor of Arts in English Literature and History from La Trobe University, as well as an Honours degree in Literary Studies from Monash University. Her research interests are women writers and ecocriticism, as well as representations of trauma in narratives.

Dai-An Le is a student who could probably be a professional poker player if she harnessed her ability to bluff through life. Somehow, she was the highest placed Monash student for the 2018 Monash Undergraduate Creative Writing Prize. Now people think she can write. Oops.

Eleanor Maher writes fiction and narrative non-fiction focusing on place and the personal. In 2018 she completed an honours thesis in literary studies at Monash University on the subject of ghosts.

Mara Papavassiliou is a paralegal and copyrighter from Perth. She has written countless judicial case summaries, legal briefs and branding guides for community legal centres and not-for-profits and is now making the foray into creative fiction. In her spare time Mara volunteers at a public interest environmental legal centre and is a member of the International Union for the Conservation of Nature. Her work has previously been featured in *Pelican* magazine, where she was also News Editor.

Emily Riches is a writer from the Northern Rivers of New South Wales who lives in Sydney. She won Monash's Undergraduate Creative Writing Prize in 2014 and has since been published in *Seizure Online*, the *Newcastle Short Story Award Anthology* and *Southerly*.

Chloe Riley completed an honours arts degree in creative writing at Monash University in 2016. She was first published in *Verge 2017: Chimera* and was featured in the New Zealand journal *Aotearotica*'s fifth volume in 2018. She is writing a lesbian novella set in Victoria's high country in the 1950s as part of a masters degree.

N'Gadie Roberts is a 22-year-old writer. She was born in Sierra Leone but grew up in Perth, Western Australia. Earlier this year, she completed her Honours in English and Cultural Studies at The University of Western Australia. Her creative writing dissertation (a collection of short stories) explored the use of the uncanny to represent experiences of trauma in contemporary fiction. 'The Harvest Man' is one of these stories. She enjoys playing table tennis, walking along the beach, and watching 80s horror flicks. She also manages an Instagram account *Olayinka_* where she publishes poetry and micro fiction.

Shamina Rozario is an avid writer and environmental activist who has completed an honours degree on the work of American poet Elizabeth Bishop. Her poetry is inspired by psychodynamics and the cryptic and uncanny nature of dream material.

Kishore Ryan is a writer, composer and drummer. 'I Purchased Two Donkeys' appears in *Verge 2019* as a poem, but it was recently performed as a libretto in Kishore's composition of the same name for percussion, electronics and pre-recorded voice. The piece was premiered by Texan percussion trio Line Upon Line at the 2018 Bendigo International Festival of Exploratory Music.

Gary Smith teaches in the arts communication school at Deakin University and has had several poems, short fiction and feature articles published. He has been a guest performer at the Melbourne Writers Festival, Montsalvat Poetry Festival and other events, and is a past secretary of Melbourne Poets Union.

Rebecca Starford is a second-year PhD candidate in Creative Writing at the University of Queensland. Her research interests include the uncanny and haunting in contemporary Australian literature, and the creative component of her thesis, a novel entitled *The Visitor*, investigates the literary representation of the uncanny in contemporary Australian fiction. Rebecca is the author of the memoir *Bad Behaviour* (Allen & Unwin) and forthcoming novel *The Handler* (2020), and is the publishing director of *Kill Your Darlings* literary magazine.

Hannah C. van Didden tends to words, projects, children, and chickens in Perth, WA. You will find other pieces of her in places such as *Crannóg, Southerly, Breach, Atticus Review, Southword Journal,* and her blog, *thirtyseven.*

lou verga is an English language teacher from Melbourne's north. He has recently completed an MA literary thesis, which focuses on camp aestheticism in marginalised suburban settings.

Jeanne Viray is a Manila-born writer based in Melbourne. Her work has appeared in *DjedPress,* Issue 12 of *F*EMSZINE,* Monash University's *Lot's Wife,* and the Monash Creative Writing Club's *Incisors & Grinders.* She is currently studying law and arts, and is working on more experimental writing and speculative fiction.

Carl Voller is studying for a BA in education and creative writing at the University of the Sunshine Coast. He is writing his first novel, which merges magic realism, crime and personal experience. As a Queensland detective, he spent most of 32 years investigating juvenile crime and child abuse. He was published in the 2017 USC anthology *Arrhythmia.*

Michael Walton is an emerging writer and spoken word performer, based in Melbourne. He is currently studying literature, archaeology and physics at Monash University. His work, both poetry and prose, has been published previously in the student anthology *Incisors & Grinders,* which can be found on WordPress at incisorsgrinders.wordpress.com.

Aileen Westbrook lives in Sydney near the Parramatta River. She is currently doing a BA in creative writing and ancient history at Macquarie University. She was winner of the 2018 Monash Undergraduate Prize for Creative Writing.

Gavin Yates is a doctoral candidate in creative writing at Monash University. His thesis charts the history and use of Surrealism in Australian poetry. Gavin's writing has been published in many journals including *Cordite Poetry Review*, *Flash Cove*, *Foam:e*, *Inverted Syntax*, *Otoliths*, *Tincture*, and *Westerly*, among others.